He turned off the Christmas tree lights, then together they climbed the stairs.

As always the first thing Melissa did when she reached the top of the stairs was go into the boys' bedroom to see that they were still peacefully sleeping.

Henry followed her in and a soft smile played on his face as he looked first at Joey and then at James. That smile, filled with such love, with such tenderness created a warmth inside her.

She would never have to worry about her sons being loved. If anything ever happened to her Henry would make sure they not only had what they needed to survive, but that their world would be filled with the love he refused to believe in for himself.

"Melissa." He grabbed her hand as they left the room.

She knew immediately what he wanted—and what she wanted from him.

Dear Reader,

Christmas is my favorite holiday of the year. I begin decorating my house in November and I'm not satisfied until the entire house breathes with the spirit of Christmas. I love the scent of pine in the air, the glow of twinkling lights on the tree and the warmth that fills my heart.

During this time of year I find myself smiling more, humming carols under my breath, baking goodies for friends and neighbors and picking up special gifts that will bring a smile to somebody's face.

No other holiday speaks to me more of love and family and surprises. Writing *The Cowboy's Secret Twins* reminded me of all the wonderful feelings that Christmas evokes.

I hope when you read the book it will bring to mind memories of Christmases past, of laughter and family and, of course, love.

Happy reading!

Carla Cassidy

CARLA CASSIDY

The Cowboy's Secret Twins

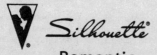

Silhouette®

Romantic

SUSPENSE

 SILHOUETTE BOOKS

Recycling programs
for this product may
not exist in your area.

ISBN-13: 978-0-373-27654-7

THE COWBOY'S SECRET TWINS

Copyright © 2009 by Carla Bracale

Books by Carla Cassidy

Silhouette Romantic Suspense

†The Delaney Heirs
††Cherokee Corners
‡Wild West Bodyguards

CARLA CASSIDY

is an award-winning author who has written more than fifty novels for Silhouette Books. In 1995, she won Best Silhouette Romance from *RT BOOK Reviews* for *Anything for Danny*. In 1998, she also won a Career Achievement Award for Best Innovative Series from *RT BOOK Reviews*.

Carla believes the only thing better than curling up with a good book to read is sitting down at the computer with a good story to write. She's looking forward to writing many more books and bringing hours of pleasure to readers.

Chapter 1

Melissa Monroe couldn't help but wonder if she was making a huge mistake. A fierce case of déjà vu filled her as she drove the Texas road. The lonely highway, the snow coming down from the overcast sky and the Christmas carols playing on the car radio all evoked memories of the last time Melissa had driven on this particular road.

It had been just a little over a year ago, only at that time the snow hadn't been comprised of pretty little flakes lazily drifting down, but rather a blizzard white-out condition that had eventually forced her to pull over.

A sexy stranger in tight jeans and a cowboy hat had rescued her. He'd told her his name was James and they'd ridden out the storm together in a vacant farmhouse.

It had been a wild and crazy night and she'd acted completely out of character. The consequences of her actions that night were in two car seats in the back.

Joey and James, who were a little over four months old, had been completely unplanned and unexpected, but since the moment she'd realized she was pregnant, they had been desperately wanted and loved.

She glanced back now to check on them and smiled. Snug as bugs they were in their little blue coats and matching hats. They'd been sleeping for the better part of an hour and Melissa hoped to get where she was going before they woke up demanding another meal.

Thirty minutes ago she'd passed the place in the road where she'd had to pull over during the storm a year ago. It was just outside the small town of Rockport, Texas. She was now ten minutes from the Texas town of Dalhart and her final destination.

On that night a year ago she'd been on her way from her home in Amarillo to visit a friend in Oklahoma. Tonight she was on her way to someplace just on the other side of Dalhart.

Tightening her hands on the steering wheel, she hoped she wasn't on some kind of a wild-goose chase. Suddenly all kinds of doubts crashed through her mind. Maybe she was a fool to trust her cyber friend, a woman she'd never met in person but had bonded with over the past year in a chat room for single moms.

MysteryMom had been a source of support, information and friendship over the past year. She'd helped Melissa through the difficult pregnancy. Then once the twins were born she'd been a font of advice on everything from colic to diaper rash.

MysteryMom and Melissa's best friend, Caitlin, were the only two people on earth who knew about the circumstances of the twins' conception.

Melissa suspected that MysteryMom had given her directions to her place, that she was bringing Melissa to her home for a face-to-face meeting and to spend the holidays together.

For the past couple of weeks Melissa had been depressed. Christmas was only four days away—the twins' first Christmas—and she hadn't even had any extra cash to buy a tree or a single present.

She'd always dreamed of giving her children the kind of Christmas she'd never had, with family gathered close and laughter in the air. It wasn't all about a lack of money that had depressed her, but certainly financial worries played a role.

She'd been working at building her own interior design business when she'd found herself pregnant. The pregnancy had been difficult and the business had fallen by the wayside. Since the twins' birth Melissa had been living on her savings, which were dwindling fast.

It had been all she could handle to take care of newborns, but after the first of the year she was determined to somehow provide for them and delve back into her work.

She slowed as she reached the Dalhart city limits. According to the directions MysteryMom had sent her she was to turn off the main highway and onto a country road approximately ten miles from where she was now.

With a new burst of nervous tension kicking up inside her, she pulled into a restaurant parking lot and grabbed her cell phone from her purse and punched in Caitlin's number.

"Are you there yet?" Caitlin asked when she answered.

"According to the map I'm about fifteen minutes from the place," Melissa replied.

"How's the weather? I heard they were calling for snow."

"It's been spitting a bit, but nothing to worry me," Melissa replied.

"I don't know why you just didn't plan on coming to my place for Christmas instead of taking off on this adventure of yours."

Melissa smiled into the phone. "You're going to have so many fancy parties to attend, the last thing you need is me and the boys hanging around." Caitlin was single and gorgeous and working up the corporate ladder at blinding speed. "Besides, look what happened the last time I was on my way to visit you."

"It's not my fault you got stuck in a blizzard and then decided to kick it with some sexy stranger."

"True, it wasn't your fault. I've decided it was all Tom's fault," Melissa replied and tried to ignore the faint pang of her heart at the thought of her ex-boyfriend.

"Ah, don't even mention that snake's name," Caitlin replied. "I thought he was a creep when you first starting dating him and he definitely proved me right."

"Water under the bridge," Melissa replied. "Anyway, I just wanted to check in with you and let you know I'm almost there."

"You'll call me when you arrive? Tell me all about this MysteryMom of yours?"

"Definitely."

"And, Melissa, I hope you have an amazing Christmas. You deserve it."

Melissa put her cell phone back in her purse and pulled her car back on the road. Dusk was falling and she was eager to get to her destination before dark.

As she drove her mind filled with thoughts of Tom Watters. She'd thought they'd marry and build a family together and after two years of dating she'd begun to press him about setting a wedding date. He'd finally told her there wasn't going to be a wedding, that for the past six months he'd been involved with another woman, one who was much sexier, much more a woman than Melissa.

Once again she clenched her hands on the steering wheel as she thought of that moment. She'd immediately made plans to visit Caitlin, needing to get away from her dismal apartment and all reminders of Tom.

Reeling not only with a broken heart, but also with a damaged ego, she'd been easy pickings for the handsome stranger who had come to her aid.

Her cheeks burned hot as she remembered that night of unexpected passion. James had looked at her with such desire. He'd made her feel so sexy, so wanted. She'd never before experienced that kind of wild abandon and suspected she'd never experience it again.

She cast all these thoughts aside as she drew nearer to the road her directions told her to take. As she left the small town of Dalhart behind, she spied the highway sign where she needed to turn.

In approximately ten miles she should be at the destination that she suspected was MysteryMom's home. Excitement danced in her chest as she thought of finally coming face-to-face with the woman who had been not only a friend, but also a surrogate mom through the trials and tribulations of being a single new mother to twins.

If she didn't like the looks of the place she'd turn around and make the two-and-a-half-hour drive back home. If she got any bad vibes at all, she'd just drive away. There was no way she'd put her babies or herself at risk.

The first surprise was the enormous stone monuments that marked the entry to the address she sought. The second surprise was when she drove down the tree-lined narrow drive and got her first glimpse of the house. No, *house* was too plain a word for the mansion that rose into view.

The two-story home was as big as a hotel, with several equally impressive outbuildings. Lights spilled with a cheerful welcome from several of the windows as the evening had begun to thicken with night shadows.

"Oh, my goodness," she whispered to herself. The whole place breathed money.

As she drove up the circular driveway she saw that one of the outbuildings was a stable and she was more convinced than ever that this was MysteryMom's house. MysteryMom had mentioned that she loved working with horses.

She parked the car and glanced into the backseat where Joey was awake. Of the two boys, Joey was the most laid-back. He rarely fussed and seemed content to take life as it came at him.

On the other hand, James was a handful. Demanding and impatient, he was the first to set up a frustrated cry if he needed a diaper change or a meal or if she took away his beloved rattle. But, he also had begun to belly laugh when happy and the sound of it never failed to delight her.

She looked at Joey, who gazed at her with bright blue eyes. "Are you ready to go meet Mommy's new friend?" she asked. He waved his arms as if to show his excitement.

As she got out of the car she realized it had grown darker, as if night hadn't just stealthily approached but had rather slammed down without warning.

She opened the door to the backseat and first un-buckled Joey and pulled him up on her hip, then went to the other door and did the same with James. In the past four months she'd become quite adept at not only carrying both boys, but also her purse and a diaper bag all at the same time.

The cold air chased her to the front door, where she managed to use her toe to knock. Her heart hammered with excitement as she waited for MysteryMom to answer. When the door opened her excitement transformed to stunned surprise.

He filled the doorway with his broad shoulders and lean hips, and his blue eyes widened with the same shock that she felt. His gaze swept over the two babies in her arms and his face paled.

James.

For a moment her mind refused to accept what she saw. "Henry? Who's here?" a feminine voice called from somewhere in the house.

Two thoughts flew into Melissa's head. Apparently his name wasn't James and he must be married. Oh, God, this was all a mistake. A terrible mistake.

Before she could take a step backward, before she could even move a muscle, a ping sounded next to her and the wood of the doorjamb splintered apart.

Everything seemed to happen in slow motion. Another ping resounded and James or Henry or whatever his name was leaned forward, grabbed her and pulled her inside the house. He slammed the door behind them.

"Call the sheriff," he yelled. "Somebody is shooting at the house." He opened a drawer in the ornate sideboard in the entry, pulled out a gun, then without a backward glance at her, disappeared out the front door.

Melissa stood in the center of the entry, her heart

banging frantically. Mistake. This was all some sort of horrible mistake.

What kind of a man was her babies' father that somebody shot at the house the minute he'd opened his door? Was he a drug dealer? A criminal of some kind?

As Joey and James began to cry, Melissa fought back tears of her own.

Henry Randolf clung to the shadows of the house as he tried to discern exactly where the shooter might be. He thought the attack had come from the stand of trees directly in front of the house.

As he moved forward he tried not to think about the woman who had appeared on his doorstep. Melissa, that was her name. She'd crossed his thoughts often over the past year, but he couldn't think about her now or the two babies she held in her arms. He couldn't afford to get distracted while somebody with a gun was on his property.

One problem at a time, he told himself. The shooter first, then he'd have to figure out what to do about his unexpected visitor.

He clenched his gun tightly as he worked his way to the stand of trees, listening for a sound, seeking a shadow that would indicate where the attacker might be. As he thought of how close those bullets had come to Melissa and those babies, a slow seething rage built up inside him.

This wasn't the first time he'd been shot at in the past week. Three days ago he'd been riding his horse across the pasture and somebody had taken a potshot at him. His mount had reared and taken off for the stables as Henry had pulled his gun to defend himself from the unknown.

He was still outside checking the area when the sheriff's car pulled up. Sheriff Jimmy Harrick lumbered out of his patrol car like a sleepy bear exiting a favorite cave. He pulled his collar up against the cold night air as Henry approached him.

"I've checked the area. There's nobody around now. The shots came from that stand of trees over there but it's too dark to see if there's any shell casings or evidence."

He pointed toward the house. "Let's go inside and talk." Henry didn't wait for a reply but headed for the door. He hadn't felt the cold when he'd first burst outside, but now the damp December air seeped into his bones.

"Got company?" Jimmy asked as they passed the older model car in the driveway.

"Yeah, an old friend." Henry's stomach kicked with nerves as he thought of the woman who had stood on his doorstep carrying twins who looked remarkably like he had when he'd been a baby.

Damn, what mess had he gotten himself into? He had a feeling his life was about to get extremely complicated.

As he and the sheriff walked into the living room he saw Melissa seated next to his mother on the sofa, each of them with a baby in their arms.

Melissa's blue eyes were wide with fear. He couldn't blame her. There was nothing like a welcoming committee of bullets to put that expression in a woman's eyes.

Henry tore his gaze from Melissa and focused on the sheriff. "Something's got to be done, Jimmy. This is the second time somebody has taken potshots at me in the past week."

Jimmy shoved his meaty hands in his pockets and rocked back on his heels. "I'm not sure what to do about it, Henry. There's no question that you've made some enemies with your decision to run for mayor."

"And so it's okay for somebody to try to kill me? Because they don't like my politics?" Henry was acutely aware of Melissa listening to every word, watching him with those amazing eyes of hers.

Jimmy pulled his hands out of his pockets. "Now, you know that's not what I'm saying," he protested. "I'm going back out there with my flashlight and I'll take a look around, then I'll head back to town and start asking questions. I'll let you know if I find anything. If I don't then I'll give you a call sometime tomorrow."

"Fine," Henry said curtly. He knew nothing more could be done tonight and in any case he was having a difficult time thinking about anything but the woman who sat next to his mother.

He walked Jimmy to the door, then closed and locked it and drew a deep breath to steady himself. How had she found him? They'd only exchanged first names on that crazy night they'd shared a little over a year ago and he hadn't even given her his real first name.

And then there were those babies. Henry had decided he was never going to marry and he'd certainly never planned to be a father, but there was little question in his mind about the paternity of those twins. Now he had to figure out what he was going to do about it.

He returned to the living room, where the two women on the sofa didn't appear to have moved, although Melissa and the two little boys no longer wore their coats.

His mother had that look on her face she used to get when he was a kid and had done something he knew he shouldn't do. He definitely had some explaining to do.

She stood and walked over to him and thrust the baby she held into his arms. "I'm retiring to my room. It appears you and Melissa have a lot to talk about."

The little boy smelled of baby powder and gazed up at him with curious blue eyes. As Henry stared down at him the little boy's lips curved up in a sweet smile.

"That's Joey," Melissa said. "And I have James." She said the name with forced emphasis and he remembered that the night they'd been together he'd told her his name was James.

That night he hadn't wanted to be the wealthy Henry James Randolf III. He'd just wanted to be an ordinary cowboy named James. "My name is Henry. Henry James Randolf," he said.

As he looked at her several things struck him. She was still as pretty as he'd remembered her with her long blond hair and those big blue eyes, but she seemed tired and stressed.

Her cheeks grew pink beneath his scrutiny. "I don't quite know what to say. I didn't expect you."

He frowned and tightened his grip on Joey, who wiggled like a little worm. "What do you mean, you didn't expect me? You came here. You knocked on my door. Who else would you be expecting?" He sat in a chair across from the sofa as Joey leaned his head against his chest. To Henry's surprise his heart knocked hard.

"I thought I was coming to spend the holiday with a woman I met last year on the computer." Once again her cheeks warmed with color. "We met in a chat room for single pregnant women and she's been a wonderful source of support through my pregnancy and single parenting. She goes by the name of MysteryMom. She gave me this address, e-mailed me directions and told me to come here."

He eyed her suspiciously. The story certainly didn't have any ring of truth to it. "And how did she find me?"

Melissa raised a hand that trembled slightly to tuck a strand of shiny hair behind her ear. "I don't know. When we first got close I told her about the blizzard in Rockport and you coming to my rescue. All I knew about you was that your name was James and that you drove a black pickup with a license plate number that started with tin."

TIN-MAN, that's what his plate read. An old girl-friend who had proclaimed that he had no heart had dared him to get the personalized plate, and he never backed down from a dare.

"When I first realized I was pregnant," she continued, "I went back to Rockport and asked around about you, but nobody had any clue who you might be. Somebody tried to kill you."

He blinked at the unexpected change of topic. "I think it was a warning, not a real attempt on my life. Our current mayor was diagnosed with cancer and has decided to resign. The city council has called an emergency election to be held in two months. I decided to run for the position and somebody apparently doesn't like my politics."

James began to fuss, waving his fists in the air and kicking his legs. "They're hungry," Melissa said. "If you could just show me to the kitchen, I'll fix them bottles, then we'll be on our way."

"On your way? You can't leave now," he protested. "It's dark and getting later by the minute and I don't know if the person who fired that gun earlier is really gone from the area." He stood with Joey in his arms. "You'll stay here tonight and we can discuss everything further in the morning."

She stood and gazed at him with somber eyes. "You haven't even questioned if they're yours or not."

For the first time since he'd opened his door to her, he offered her a smile. "They look just like me. They even have my cleft chin. And I know we used no protection that night."

"I'm not here to cause you any trouble," she replied.

Henry nodded, although he wasn't so sure about that. "Let's go into the kitchen and get those bottles ready," he said.

Time would tell if she had really been led to his

doorstep by some mystery cyber friend or if she was just another woman who had recognized who he was on the night of the blizzard and had found a way to cash in on the Randolf fortune.

Chapter 2

Melissa snuggled down in the bed in a guest room fit for a princess. The twins were sound asleep in an old playpen that Henry had found in the attic. It had been dusted off and the padding covered with a crisp, clean sheet. The boys were clad in their pajamas and sleeping beneath a cashmere throw that was as soft as a cloud.

She'd called Caitlin just to let her friend know that everything was all right and that it hadn't been Mystery-Mom's home she'd come to, but rather the man who was the father of her boys. She'd promised to let Caitlin know everything that happened when she returned home in the morning.

She was exhausted now, but sleep refused to come.

The night had been filled with far too many surprises. The first had certainly been the sight of Henry as he'd opened the door. The second had been the bullets that had come precariously close to both her and her babies.

Even after the trauma of the shooting had passed she hadn't been able to get a read on Henry. He'd said little as he'd helped her bottle-feed the boys. She knew he had to be as stunned to see her as she'd been to see him.

They hadn't spoken much, just attended to the boys' needs, then he'd shown her to her room for the night with the promise that they'd talk further in the morning.

She didn't know what would happen. She had no idea what to expect from him, if he intended to be part of the boys' lives or not.

She'd resigned herself at the time of their birth to the fact that Joey and James wouldn't know their real father. At least now she wouldn't have to tell them the humiliating story of how she'd gotten pregnant by a stranger in a vacant farmhouse during the middle of a snowstorm.

MysteryMom must have somehow traced him with the partial license plate letters Melissa had mentioned. She obviously had resources Melissa didn't have. If MysteryMom had hoped for some kind of happy ending for Melissa, she was functioning in the world of make-believe.

Despite the intimate night they'd shared, Melissa and Henry didn't know each other at all. He hadn't even given her his real name that night.

Certainly he was in a social position to date all kinds

of sophisticated, successful women. And the last thing Melissa was looking for was a man in her life.

Tom's betrayal still burned bright in her heart and if that wasn't enough, she had two little boys to raise. She didn't want a man. She didn't want anything from Henry, except for him to be a father for her boys.

She'd been hoping to spend Christmas someplace where the spirit of the holiday was everywhere. There was no sign of Christmas in the Randolf home and in any case she didn't belong here.

First thing in the morning she'd be on her way back home to her little apartment and maybe on the way home she'd stop at a discount store and buy one of those little metal trees in celebration of the twins' first Christmas.

She finally fell asleep and dreamed of that night with Henry in front of the fire he'd built to warm them through the snowy night. The heat of the flames had been nothing compared to the fire in his kisses, the warmth of his hands on her body.

When she woke up bright sunshine drifted through her bedroom window, not the faint light of dawn she was used to, but full sunlight that let her know it was late.

The boys!

She shot up and looked at the playpen. It was empty. She jumped out of bed and yanked on her robe. Henry had gotten her suitcase from the trunk of her car the night before despite her protests that the gunman might still be out there lying in wait for him. She'd held her breath until he was back in the house safe and sound.

Now her breath caught once again in her throat as she raced out of the bedroom and down the grand staircase to the lower level of the house.

She heard voices coming from the formal dining room and headed there, her heart beating frantically as all kinds of irrational fears whirled through her head. She flew into the room and stopped short.

The boys were in their car seats on the polished mahogany wood of the huge table. Henry's mother, Mary, stood in front of them, shaking a rattle at first one, then at the other as they bubbled with laughter.

"Melissa," Mary said with a smile that faltered as Melissa sagged against the doorjamb. "Oh, dear, we frightened you, didn't we?"

"I woke up and they were gone. I wasn't sure what to think." Melissa's heart slowed its frantic pace.

"It was Henry's idea really," Mary said. "You looked so tired last night and he thought it would be nice if you got to sleep in a bit this morning. So we sneaked into your room around dawn and grabbed these two little bundles of love and brought them down here. We gave them each a bottle and then I gave them a little sponge bath and changed their clothes. I hope you don't mind."

Melissa wanted to be angry that they'd obviously riffled through the diaper bag and taken her boys from their bed. But the look on Mary's face as she gazed at the twins made it impossible for Melissa to maintain anger. Besides, if she were perfectly honest with herself the extra couple of hours of sleep had been glorious.

"You know, I never thought I'd live to see grand-babies. Henry is quite the confirmed bachelor so I'd resigned myself to the fact that there would probably never be grandchildren." She smiled at the twins. "But these two are like gifts from heaven."

Melissa smiled. "You haven't changed one of their messy diapers yet. That might change your mind about gifts from heaven."

Mary laughed. "Oh good, you have a sense of humor. I'm so glad. And now if you'll get dressed I'll have Etta make you some breakfast. Henry and I have already eaten."

"Oh, that's not necessary," Melissa replied. "I'm not much of a breakfast person and besides, I'd like to get back on the road as soon as possible." She not only wanted to get back to Amarillo, but she was still deter-mined to stop someplace on the way home and pick up a few things to bring Christmas to her tiny apartment.

At that moment Henry appeared in the opposite doorway. He seemed bigger than life, his presence sucking some of the oxygen out of the air.

He looked like the rugged, handsome cowboy she'd met on the road that night. Clad in a pair of fitted jeans and a flannel shirt that emphasized the width of his broad shoulders, he let his gaze sweep the length of her before he smiled and said good morning. Even though he smiled, his eyes remained shuttered, enigmatic.

Melissa was suddenly aware of the fact that her robe was tatty and frayed and her hair was probably sticking out in every direction. She hadn't even washed her face before hurrying down the stairs.

"I'm just going to run upstairs and shower. I'll be right back."

"When you come back down I'd like to have a talk with you," Henry said.

She nodded and backed out of the dining room then escaped back up the stairs. There had been an edge in Henry's tone of voice when he'd said he wanted to talk to her that worried her.

This whole trip had been a nightmare. The unexpected presence of a man she'd never thought she'd see again, bullets splintering a door and now the promise of a conversation she had a feeling she didn't want to have.

He was probably going to tell her to take her babies and leave, that being a dad didn't fit into his lavish single lifestyle. And even though that was fine with her, it made her heart hurt just a little bit for her sons.

She knew what it was like to grow up without a father. She remembered the empty ache his absence had created inside her and she certainly hadn't consciously chosen that for her boys.

Minutes later, as she stood under a hot spray of water she found herself again wondering what MysteryMom had hoped to accomplish by leading her here. Of course it would be nice for the boys to have a father in their lives. She wanted that for them. But she wasn't in control of Henry's reaction to instant parenthood.

Mary had said he was a confirmed bachelor. It was definitely possible a bachelor wouldn't want to be saddled with two little boys who required a lot of time and attention.

By the time she'd finished her shower and dressed, nervous energy bounced around in her stomach. She certainly didn't know Henry well enough to second-guess what he might want to discuss with her, but it didn't take a rocket scientist to know that it had something to do with Joey and James.

Despite the night of desire they'd shared, since the moment she'd arrived at this mansion Henry frightened her more than a little bit. Oh, she wasn't physically frightened of him. What scared her most was the fear of him rejecting his sons, sons that he'd never wanted and had never asked for.

When she returned downstairs Mary had the boys on their tummies on a blanket in the living room. She smiled at Melissa. "That James, he's a feisty one, isn't he? He reminds me of Henry when he was a baby. Demanding and impatient, there's going to be no holding him back when he starts to walk."

James arched his back, raised himself up and grinned at Melissa, as if relishing the very idea of being independent and mobile. Meanwhile, Joey rolled over onto his back, perfectly content to play with his fingers.

"It must be hard, being a single parent to twins," Mary said.

"I manage okay," Melissa replied with a touch of defensiveness.

"I'm sure you do, dear. Henry is waiting for you in the study," Mary said. "It's down the hall and the first door on your right."

Melissa nodded and with one last look at her contented boys, she went down the hall to the study. The door was closed and she knocked on it with a gentle tap.

She heard him tell her to come in and she opened the door. Henry sat behind a massive mahogany desk and although he smiled at her as she stepped into the room, it did nothing to alleviate her nervousness.

The study was as beautifully appointed as the other rooms in the house. A stone fireplace took up one wall and floor-to-ceiling bookcases filled another. "Melissa, please have a seat." He gestured to the chair in front of the desk. She sank down and tried not to be intimidated by the surroundings, by him.

"Mom said you were eager to get on the road and head home, but I wanted to talk to you about the possibility of you staying through Christmas," he said.

"Oh, I'm not sure…" She paused as he held up a hand to stop whatever she was about to say.

"We're forever linked now by those boys and despite the fact that we had that night together, I don't know anything about you."

Oh, but he did, she thought. He knew she liked to be kissed just below her ear, that if he stroked her breasts she moaned deep in the back of her throat. A whisper of longing swept through her as she remembered that night and him. She forced herself to focus on what he was saying.

"We stopped having anything to celebrate at Christmastime three years ago when my father unexpectedly died of a heart attack on Christmas Day. Since then Christmas each year has slid by with little celebration in this house. But this year we have something to celebrate. The twins. I'd like to give them a terrific first Christmas, so please tell me you'll stay."

Her first instinct was relief, that he wasn't casting the boys out and that he apparently wanted to get to know them better. Still, there was one thing that made her relief short-lived. "I have to be honest. I haven't forgotten those bullets that flew when I arrived here," she said. "I don't want to put Joey and James in harm's way." She fought against a shiver as she thought of the bullets that had come far too close to them the night before.

"I feel more comfortable with you here rather than going back outside," he replied. "Somebody is being a nuisance, obviously attempting to make me rethink my position in running for mayor, but I won't let any harm come to you or the children."

She considered his words thoughtfully and believed him. There was something solid about him, a strength in his eyes that let her know he wouldn't allow danger to come to her or her babies.

He was their father and all he was asking was for her to remain a couple more days. Surely there was no harm in that, in giving him and his mother the first Christmas with the boys.

"Okay," she finally replied. "We'll stay through the holiday." She had no idea if it were the right thing to do or if it was possible she was making a terrible mistake.

A wave of satisfaction swept through Henry at her reply. From the moment she'd stepped into the study he'd smelled her, a familiar scent of fresh flowers with a hint of vanilla. It was the same fragrance she'd worn the night they'd been snowbound together and it stirred all kinds of crazy memories inside him.

As she stood and tucked a strand of hair behind her ear he remembered how soft, how silky her hair had been beneath his touch. That wasn't all he remembered. There was the taste of her mouth open to his, the spill of her warm, full breasts into his palms and the moans that had escaped her at his every touch. Desire slammed into his stomach, hot and wild and completely unexpected.

He had no idea if he trusted her, hadn't spent enough time with her to know if he even liked her, but that didn't stop him from wanting a repeat of what they'd shared on that snowy night.

"Good. We'll make it a Christmas to remember," he said and stood.

She backed toward the doorway, as if eager to escape him. "I'm going to take the boys upstairs for their morning naps. I'll see you later."

"Melissa," he said, stopping her before she could

disappear from the room. "I don't even know your last name."

She smiled, the first real smile he'd seen from her, and the gesture lit her up from the inside out. "Monroe. Melissa Monroe."

The minute Melissa left the study Henry leaned back in his chair and gazed thoughtfully out the window. From this vantage point he could see the carriage house in the distance. It was a two-bedroom self-contained cottage that was occasionally used as guest quarters.

Henry had been living there before his father's death. His heart constricted as he thought about his dad. Not a day went by that Henry didn't miss him. Big Henry, as he'd been called, had not only been father, but he'd also been friend and mentor to his only son. The two of them had worked side by side running Randolf Enterprises, which was comprised of not only the ranch but also oil wells and enormous financial holdings.

There were people in town who were threatened not only by the financial power Henry possessed, but also by his decision to run for the position of mayor and clean up the corruption he knew ran rife through the city offices of Dalhart.

He had a couple suspicions of who might have taken those shots at him, but suspicions didn't work for an arrest. He also suspected that whoever had shot at him hadn't really tried to kill him but rather was just warning him, hoping he'd decide not to run for mayor.

Those gunshots didn't scare him half as much as the

idea that Melissa might not allow him to be as big a part of the boys' lives as he wanted.

"Henry?" His mother entered the study, her features worried. "Is she going to stay?" She sat in front of him in the chair that Melissa had vacated.

"She didn't tell you?"

"I was in the kitchen speaking with Etta about dinner. Melissa took the babies and went upstairs before I got a chance to ask her."

"She's staying until after Christmas." He leaned forward. "I don't quite know what to make of her. The story she told me about some cyber friend giving her directions here sounded more than a little bit shady."

"You think she's after money?"

"It certainly looks like she could use it." He frowned as he thought of the rusted old car out front, the frayed robe that had hugged her curves that morning.

Mary leaned back in her chair and folded her hands in her lap. "You want to tell me how this happened?"

Henry grinned at her. "You need a lesson in biology?"

She scowled at him. "You know what I mean, Henry. I've never heard you mention this woman's name before and yet she shows up here with two babies who are obviously yours."

"Remember the blizzard we had at the beginning of December last year? The night I couldn't get home from Hilary's because of the whiteout conditions?"

"That was the night you broke up with that woman."

Henry nodded. "I was on my way home when the

conditions got impossible to drive in. As I pulled over to the side of the road I saw another car there and Melissa was inside. I had no idea how bad the weather was going to get and I'd just passed the old Miller place and knew it was vacant, so I got her out of her car and we holed up there for the night."

Mary raised a hand. "That's all I need to know about the particulars. Is it possible she knew who you were?"

Henry pulled a hand down his lower jaw. "I don't know. I suppose anything is possible. I've always been so careful. I've always recognized how vulnerable I was to gold diggers."

Mary arched an eyebrow upward. "Need we mention Hilary's name?"

Henry smiled as he thought of the woman he'd been dating and had broken up with the afternoon of the blizzard that had brought him and Melissa together.

"Hilary might be a gold digger, but she never kept that fact a secret," he replied. Since the day of their breakup the attractive brunette hadn't stopped waging her battle to become Mrs. Henry Randolf III. She called him or came by at least once a week in an attempt to seduce him back into her arms.

Mary straightened her back and sniffed indignantly. "That woman couldn't wait to marry you and have me shut up in a nursing home someplace. The evil witch."

And that had been the very reason Henry had broken up with Hilary. It was at the moment she mentioned that she thought it would be uncomfortable living with Mary and that Hilary had been searching for a nice nursing home for the older woman when Henry had recognized there would never be a future with her and certainly not a marriage.

"You don't have to worry about that," he said to his mother. Once again he leaned back in his chair and cast his gaze out the window.

"I never really thought about having kids," he said softly. "But now that they exist I want them here with me. I want them to grow up here on the ranch and learn the family business. I want to teach them like Dad taught me."

"Aren't you forgetting one little thing? Melissa might not want to move here. She might have a perfectly fine life, perhaps with a boyfriend or family of her own."

Henry frowned thoughtfully. "I find that hard to believe. I mean, according to her story she took off from her home to meet some cyber friend and spend Christmas with her. If Melissa has family or a boyfriend, why didn't she stay home to spend Christmas with them?"

"I'm sure I don't know. You know her better than I do. But, Henry, you have to remember that just because you want something doesn't mean you can have it. You're talking about a woman here, not a business deal."

Mary stood. "All I know is that I intend to enjoy each and every minute of having those babies in this house. And now I'm going to go make a shopping list. There's only two shopping days left before Christmas and suddenly I'm in the mood to shop."

She practically floated out of the study. Henry hadn't seen his mother this happy since his father had been alive.

Even though he'd had the entire night to process the fact that he was now a father, he still wasn't sure how this was all going to work. The first thing he would have to do was get to know Melissa, find out if she'd come here looking for easy street or if the story she'd told him was true.

But before he could do that he had some phone calls to make. He'd promised Melissa a Christmas to remember and Henry never broke a promise.

His mother was wrong about one thing—this *was* a business deal. Melissa had what Henry wanted and all Henry had to figure out was what price he'd have to pay to get it.

Chapter 3

Melissa stood at the window and watched as a car pulled up out front and Mary got into the car's passenger side. When the vehicle pulled away Melissa wondered if she should be doing the same thing—driving out the main gates and heading for home.

Behind her in the playpen the two boys had just fallen asleep. They usually napped for about an hour in the morning and the same amount of time in the afternoon.

Restless energy coursed through Melissa and she moved to the window on the opposite side of the room to gaze out at the pastures, corrals and outbuildings on the land. In the distance she could see what appeared to be a carriage house.

The dusting of snow that had fallen the evening before had melted beneath the warmth of the sunshine. It was a beautiful day, cold but clear.

A whisper of noise whirled her around and she saw Henry standing just outside the room in the hallway. He motioned to her and she left the room. "I thought maybe while the boys napped you might want to have a cup of coffee with me. I'd like to get to know you, Melissa."

Once again nervous energy fluttered in her chest. Of course he wanted to know her better. She was the mother of his children. "And I'd like to get to know you better," she agreed. "Coffee sounds wonderful."

She checked on the boys to make sure they were still asleep, then followed him down the staircase to the dining room where Etta, the Randolf cook, carried in a tray laden with two cups of coffee, cream and sugar and two small plates with slices of cinnamon coffee cake.

Henry introduced the older woman to Melissa. "Etta has been keeping the Randolf family well fed for the past twenty years."

"And it's been a pleasure," Etta replied. Then with a friendly smile at Melissa she turned and left the dining room.

Melissa pulled a coffee cup before her and wrapped her fingers around it. As Henry watched her she felt ill at ease and wasn't sure what to say, where to begin.

"This is awkward, isn't it?" he finally said.

She flashed him a grateful smile. At least he felt it, too. "Terribly awkward," she agreed. "I know you have no reason to believe me, but it's important to me that you know that I don't just fall into bed with strangers I meet."

She couldn't hold his gaze and instead looked down at her coffee as she continued. "That morning the man I'd been dating for two years, the man I thought I was going to marry, let me know that he had found a new girlfriend, somebody sexier than me." She felt her cheeks warm with her confession. "That night I just… It all went more than a little crazy."

He laughed, a low chuckle that was both pleasant and surprising. She looked up at him sharply, wondering if he were laughing at her.

"It seems fate had a hand in our meeting that night. I was coming home after ending a relationship with a woman I'd been dating for over a year. Maybe we were both a little reckless that night."

"But that's not who I am," she replied. "I'm usually not reckless."

He took a sip of his coffee, eyeing her over the rim of his cup. "And yet you took off with an address to an unknown place given to you by a woman you've never met before."

"A calculated risk," she replied. "If I didn't like the looks of the place when I arrived, I wasn't going to stop." She tugged on a strand of her hair in frustration. "Okay, it wasn't the brightest thing in the world to do," she conceded.

She wasn't about to tell him that it was an aching loneliness that had driven her to meet MysteryMom.

Although she loved her boys more than anything else on the face of the earth, she'd been hungry for adult conversation. The idea of spending the holiday alone had depressed her.

She reached for one of the plates and a fork. Whenever she was nervous she wanted to eat and it was impossible to ignore the heavenly scent of the cinnamon that wafted from the coffee cake.

"Okay, let's start with the basics," he said. "Henry James Randolf, thirty-five years old, rancher and oilman. I'm a Taurus. I like my steak rare and sunrise rides on my horse. I've been told that I'm stubborn but I don't necessarily see that as a fault. I'm not a big drinker but I do like a glass of scotch or brandy in the evenings. Now, your turn."

"Melissa Sue Monroe, thirty years old. I'm a Libra and I like my steak well-done. Before I got pregnant I was working to build my own interior design business. I've never been on a horse and my drink of choice is an occasional glass of wine. Oh, and I've been told I have a bit of a stubborn streak, too."

He smiled, although she noticed that the gesture didn't quite warm the blue of his eyes. "What about family?" he asked.

She shook her head and paused to take a bite of the cake. "I don't have any. My father left when I was five, told my mother he wasn't cut out for family life. I never saw him again. My mother passed away two years ago and since then it's just been me…and of course, the boys."

"You have friends who give you emotional support?"

"My best friend lives in Oklahoma, so I don't see her very often. As far as other friends, to be honest the birth of the twins has pretty much put an end to any social life for me."

"How's your interior design business?"

She considered lying. She thought about telling him that she was wildly successful, but he was obviously an intelligent man. He only had to take a glance at her car and note the worn condition of her clothing to know that the money wasn't rolling into her household.

"Nonexistent," she finally said. "The pregnancy was difficult and for the last three months of it, I couldn't work. Since then it's been just as difficult. The boys have required all my time and energy." She raised her chin. "But after the holidays I'm going to try to get back to work."

She took a sip of her coffee and wished he didn't smell exactly like she remembered from that snowy night, a scent of clean male and wintry air and a faint whisper of spicy cologne. It was a fragrance that stirred her with memories of warm hands and hot kisses.

"How have you been supporting yourself?" he asked.

"I had a small inheritance from my mother." She shifted positions beneath the intensity of his stare and took another bite of her coffee cake.

"You have a boyfriend? Somebody significant in your life?"

A small laugh burst from her. "Definitely not. The only males in my life wear diapers and drool."

This time the smile that curved his lips warmed the blue of his eyes. "At least they're cute when they drool." His smile faded. "I'm sorry I wasn't there to help through the pregnancy. I'm sorry you had to go through it all alone and I promise you won't be doing it all alone now."

She wasn't sure why his words, rather than comforting her, filled her with a new burst of apprehension. Maybe if she really knew him, knew what kind of a man he was, she wouldn't feel so worried about what he might have in mind for her and the boys.

"Having grown up without a father figure in my life, I understand how important the role of father is and will be to my boys. I want you to know that I'm open to a discussion about visitation for you," she said.

"There will be time to discuss the particulars of that over the next couple of days," he replied. He took a sip of his coffee and leaned back in his chair. "So, are you originally from Amarillo?"

She nodded. "Born and raised there." This was the kind of talk they might have had if they'd been on a date, the kind they should have had that night instead of falling on each other like two sex-starved teenagers.

"Do you have somebody special in your life? A woman you're seeing? I don't want my presence here to make any problems for you," she said.

"You don't have to worry. There's nobody special. I don't intend for there ever to be anyone special." There was a firm finality in his voice.

She took another sip of her coffee. God, the man was

so good-looking she couldn't imagine the women in the area leaving him alone. "Your mother mentioned that you were a confirmed bachelor."

"I am. The only reason I might have entertained the idea of marriage would have been to have a son to pass the ranch to when I died. You've managed to give me two without the nuisance of a marriage."

Nuisance of marriage? Funny how different they were, Melissa thought. She'd wanted to be married for a very long time, had always thought that by the time she turned thirty she'd be part of a family like she'd never had growing up.

She still hoped for that someday. The only difference her dream had from reality was that in reality her boys would have their real daddy and then maybe eventually they'd have a loving, caring stepfather.

But at the moment, any kind of relationship with a man seemed impossible. She was just too tired to even think about romance. She'd been tired for months, not that she minded. The twins were more than worth any exhaustion they caused.

"You look tired, Melissa," he said as if he'd read her thoughts. "I hope you'll take your time here and allow my mother and me to help so that you can get some extra rest. It can't be easy dealing with twins all by yourself."

"I'm fine," she assured him. "It's gotten easier since they sleep through the night most of the time now."

"Still, I hope you'll let us take some of the burden for the next couple of days."

"They aren't a burden. They're my joy," she exclaimed a bit more vehemently than the situation warranted.

He leaned forward and reached out and brushed the corner of her mouth. "You had a little cinnamon," he said as he pulled his hand back.

She grabbed a napkin and wiped her mouth and tried to ignore the electric jolt his touch had shot through her body. *He just swiped your mouth,* she told herself. A simple, casual touch and yet she felt it from head to toe.

A loud knock sounded on the front door and he pushed back from the table. "You might want to come with me to answer it," he said. "I think it's for you."

"For me? Who would be here for me?" She got up from the table and followed him to the front door.

He looked outside, then smiled and this time his smile warmed her completely. "It's Christmas, Melissa. Christmas has officially arrived at the Randolf house."

Henry opened the door to allow in the four ranch hands who maneuvered a huge evergreen tree through the door. The boughs were tied down and Hank and Tim, the ranch hands bringing up the rear, carried between them a huge pot to stand the tree in.

"It was the biggest one old man Keller had on his lot," Charlie said as they carried the tree into the living room.

"Melissa, can you help me move the coffee table?" Henry asked.

She quickly grabbed one side and he grabbed the

other. They moved the table out of the men's way. "Just set it up in the corner," he instructed.

"That's the biggest tree I've ever seen," Melissa said, her eyes round with wonder.

Henry smiled. "I told them to get the biggest one they could find. We'll decorate it this evening after dinner."

"We could string popcorn and cranberries." She flushed and shook her head as if irritated with herself. "That was silly of me. I'm sure you have lovely expensive ornaments."

He could tell she was embarrassed and he found that oddly endearing. "Actually, I've always wanted to do a tree the old-fashioned way. I think it would be fun to string popcorn and cranberries."

The look she gave him was so sweet, so grateful, that he once again felt a stir of desire deep in the pit of his stomach. When he'd brushed the trace of cinnamon from her lip moments earlier, he'd wanted to kiss it off.

He focused on watching his men wrestle the tree into the stand. Something about Melissa touched him, a vulnerability, a wistfulness in her eyes that he hadn't seen in a woman's eyes for a very long time.

He still didn't trust her. The only woman Henry really trusted was his mother, who had no ulterior motive for loving him. Any other woman he'd ever allowed close had ultimately shown herself to be more interested in the Randolf fortune than in whatever Henry could offer her as a man.

He didn't know if perhaps Melissa was just smarter

than them all and had managed to trap him like none of the other women had managed to do.

Once the men had the tree up and the ropes off, Henry introduced Melissa to them. "These are some of the best ranch hands in the state of Texas," he said. "That's Hank and Tim, Ben and Mike and Jacob and that rascal with the black hat is Charlie, my right-hand man."

Melissa's eyes had glazed over and he smiled at her. "Don't worry, there won't be a test later," he said.

She laughed and the sound of her musical laughter shot a rivulet of warmth through him. "Good, because you lost me at Hank." She smiled at all the men. "But it's nice to meet you all."

"I'll be right back," Henry said to her as the men began to head for the front door.

In the entry he touched Charlie's shoulder and motioned for Charlie to stay behind while the rest of them got back to their work.

"You heard about the shots fired last night?" he asked.

Charlie nodded. "Jimmy talked to a couple of us late yesterday evening."

"I want all of you armed while on the property until we know what's going on," Henry said. "And I'd like to work a couple of you in shifts so that somebody is always working the house. Talk to the men and see what kind of schedule you can arrange."

Charlie's eyes narrowed. "You looking for more trouble?"

Henry released a small sigh of frustration. "To be

honest, I'm not sure what I'm looking for, but twice now somebody has taken potshots at me and I don't like the idea of anyone on my property attacking me or mine."

"We'll work out a schedule and I'll get it to you this afternoon," Charlie replied.

"Thanks, Charlie. I really appreciate it," Henry replied.

"It's no problem. We can't let the boss get hurt." With these words he stepped out the door.

Henry watched him catch up to the other men. Charlie was a good worker, always pitching in for even the dirtiest jobs. When Henry had broken up with Hilary he'd worried that he was going to lose Charlie. Hilary was Charlie's sister and Henry had feared that Charlie might feel compelled to stop working for him because of sibling loyalty. But Charlie had assured him that he wasn't going anywhere and that he didn't get involved in his sister's affairs.

Henry had gotten the impression that there was no love lost between the two. In any case, he was grateful that he hadn't lost Charlie. Good workers were hard to find.

In fact, he was going to have to let Hank go. He'd noticed the tall, thin man had smelled like a brewery despite the fact it wasn't even lunchtime. Henry had already warned him twice about drinking on the job. There wouldn't be any more warnings.

He closed the front door and returned to the living room to find Melissa gone. She'd apparently gone upstairs to check on the twins. He walked over to the large floor-to-ceiling windows and gazed out to the outbuildings in the distance. The tree was only the first of the deliveries that would take place over the next two days.

The brief conversation he'd had with her over coffee had told him exactly what he needed to know. She had no family and he suspected she had few friends. That would make what he had in mind much easier. All he had to do was convince Melissa that his plan was in the best interest of them all.

He looked up as he heard the sound of her coming down the stairs, a baby on each hip. He hurried to meet her halfway and took one of the boys from her.

As he scooped the little one from her arms he tried not to notice the warmth of her body, that scent of her that half dizzied him with memories.

"Which one do I have?" he asked.

"Joey," she replied.

"How can you tell the difference?" The little boy snuggled against Henry's chest, as if aware that he was held in loving arms. Once again the heart that Henry didn't know he possessed filled with a strange wonder and a fierce sense of protectiveness.

"Once you get to know them better, it's easy to tell them apart by their personalities," she said as they hit the landing. "But the quickest way is that Joey has a tiny scar in his right eyebrow. He was reluctant to be born and the doctor had to use forceps."

Henry looked at the little boy in his arms and noticed the tiny scar at the corner of his eyebrow. Joey grinned up at him and reached for his nose. Henry laughed as he dodged the little hand.

James kicked his feet and wailed, his face turning red as Melissa wrestled with him. "He's hungry and he has no manners," she said.

"Ah, a boy after my own heart," Henry replied. "Let's go to the kitchen and get them some lunch."

The kitchen was a huge room although Henry and Mary rarely took meals there. This was Etta's space but it was also the easiest place to feed two hungry little boys.

Etta was in the process of preparing lunch, but smiled with welcome as they all entered. Henry got the car seats that were serving as high chairs and placed them in the center of the large oak table, Once the boys were settled he watched Melissa prepare two small bowls of cereal.

As she approached the table he held out his hand for one of the bowls.

"You might want to put on a hazmat suit," she warned as she gave him one of the bowls and a small baby spoon. "They not only like to eat cereal, they also like to blow it and spit it and play in it."

Feeding Joey was a pleasure like Henry had never known before. The kitchen filled with laughter as he and Melissa spooned cereal into their waiting mouths, off the front of their shirts and themselves.

"Well. this sounds like fun," Mary exclaimed as she came into the kitchen.

"Ah, the shopper is home," Henry said as he wiped off Joey's face then handed him his bottle.

"Randy is putting my purchases upstairs in my room." She smiled at Melissa. "It's been far too long since this house had such laughter in it. And the tree, it's going to be just lovely."

"Melissa thought it would be fun to string popcorn and cranberries for the tree," Henry said.

Mary clapped her hands together. "What a lovely idea. We'll have a real old-fashioned tree trimming. I'll make hot cocoa and we'll play Christmas music and have such fun."

Melissa looked from Mary to Henry. "You both are so kind," she said and once again he saw a touch of vulnerability in the depths of her eyes.

"Nonsense, you're family now," Mary replied.

But she wasn't family, Henry thought. She was still a stranger. And she would never really be family, he mentally added. Sure, he had a strong physical attraction to her and she was the mother of his boys, but she would never be anything more than that to him.

His father had spent a lot of years warning Henry about the women who would want him for his money, women like Hilary who would turn themselves into whatever he wanted or needed to access the kind of lifestyle he could provide for them. As far as his father was concerned, aside from his wife, Mary, women were cunning creatures to avoid except for the occasional physical release, and then only if protection was used.

"I was lucky, boy," his father would often say. "I was

poor as a church mouse when I met your mother. I never had to worry about if she loved me for my money or for myself. You won't have that luxury. You'll never really know if a woman loves you or your money."

He knew without a doubt that Melissa hadn't set out to seduce him that night. There was no way she could have orchestrated the blizzard and the two of them being on the road at the same time in the same place.

What he didn't know was that once fate had placed them in that position, had she recognized him and taken a calculated risk of getting pregnant? It had been a mutual seduction that night. She'd been as willing a participant as he had been.

He frowned thoughtfully as he watched her coo and sweet-talk the two little boys. But if that was the case, if she'd recognized him that night before she'd slept with him, why hadn't she contacted him the minute she realized she was pregnant? Maybe she'd been afraid he'd talk her into an abortion.

One thing was clear. Henry wanted his boys living here with him and he would achieve that goal with or without Melissa's help.

Chapter 4

The afternoon seemed to fly by. Melissa was shocked when two baby cribs were delivered and Henry had them set up in the room across from hers. And the beds weren't all. High chairs were also delivered, fancy high chairs that seated infants then changed to accommodate toddlers, along with boxes and packages in all shapes and sizes.

"This isn't necessary," she'd protested. "We're only going to be here a couple of days."

"Then things will be more comfortable for the couple of days that you're here," Henry had replied.

Dinner was a pleasant meal with the boys happily seated in their new high chairs and most of the conversation between Mary and Melissa. Henry had been quiet, watching Melissa with an enigmatic gaze that made her overly self-conscious and more than a little bit nervous.

After dinner they all gathered in the living room for the tree-trimming party. Mary supplied thick thread and needles to string the popcorn and cranberries that Etta provided, and Henry carried the two high chairs into the room and placed the boys in the seats.

"Why don't I put the lights on while you two make the garland?" Henry asked.

Mary smiled at Melissa. "He'd do anything to get out of using a needle and thread."

"Sewing is a woman's work," Henry replied.

"Stubborn and a male chauvinist, what a surprise," Melissa exclaimed.

"I'm not a male chauvinist," he protested. "I just don't like needles."

"Okay, then stubborn and a bit of a wuss," Melissa replied teasingly.

Mary laughed in delight. "Finally, a woman who can put you in your place, Henry."

Henry looked at Melissa and in the depths of his eyes she saw a flicker of heat that stirred something wild and hot inside her.

"Ouch!" she exclaimed as she pricked her finger with the needle. She instantly put her finger in her mouth and Henry's eyes flamed brighter.

"And that's why I don't like needles," he finally said and turned his attention to the string of Christmas lights.

There was definitely something between them, she thought. Something hot and hungry. She wasn't in love with him, didn't know him well enough to gauge exactly what she thought of him. But there was no denying the strong physical attraction that existed between them.

"I always wanted to do a tree like this," Mary said. "Old-fashioned and simple. Big Henry was into flash and gaudy." A soft smile curved her lips. "That man wouldn't know simple if it tapped him on the head."

"You miss him," Melissa said.

Mary leaned back against the sofa cushion, the smile still lingering on her lips. "He was stubborn as a mule, ridiculously opinionated and could make a saint weep with frustration, but yes, I miss him each and every day." She tapped her heart with a finger. "But he's still with me in here."

That's what Melissa wanted, what Mary and Big Henry had apparently shared, a love that would last through eternity. "I'm so sorry for your loss," she said and covered Mary's hand with hers.

Mary smiled and gave her hand a squeeze and then released it and began to string popcorn once again. "Thank you. I'm just sorry he's not here now to meet his grandsons. He would have been so pleased to know that there will be another generation."

"I'm going into town tomorrow and thought you might like to take the ride with me, Melissa," Henry said. "Mom can babysit the boys for an hour or so."

"I'd be happy to do that," Mary agreed.

"Oh, I don't know," Melissa said hesitantly. She'd never left the boys for a minute since their births.

"I promise I won't beat them or chain them to their beds," Mary said gently.

Melissa laughed. "That never entered my mind." She looked at Henry. "Aren't you afraid to go out? I mean it was just last night that somebody shot at you…at us."

"I won't be a prisoner in my own house," he said with a tone of steel in his voice. "Besides, I've got my men watching the grounds and we'll be safe in town. Nobody would risk trying to hurt me with so many other people around."

Melissa was torn. She was reluctant to leave the boys for any amount of time, yet there was a tiny simmer of excitement as she thought of an hour or two without them. The idea of a trip into town was appealing, but she was surprised by how cavalier he was about somebody trying to hurt him.

"I keep telling you that I don't believe my life is really in danger, that I think somebody is just trying to aggravate me, trying to manipulate me into throwing in the towel on my plans to be mayor," he said.

"Okay, I'll go with you," she finally said, unsure if it was just another reckless decision on her part.

"Good. We'll plan on going after breakfast and we'll be home before lunchtime," he replied.

"It will be fine, dear." Mary reached over and patted

Melissa's hand. "I remember the first time I left Henry with somebody. He was just about the twins' age and Big Henry had decided I needed a night out. I must have called home a dozen times to check on Henry in the two hours we were gone. Big Henry finally decided to bring me home."

Melissa smiled. "They're getting to the age where if you blink you feel like you've missed a first."

"I've already missed too many firsts," Henry said with a touch of vehemence.

He would make a good father, Melissa thought. Whenever he looked at the boys she saw a fierce love shining from his eyes. As crazy as it sounded, there was a tiny part of her that wished that same expression were in his eyes whenever he gazed at her.

She recognized the foolishness of such a wish. He was a confirmed bachelor and in any case he was the kind of man who could choose from a harem of successful, beautiful women if he ever did decide to end his bachelorhood.

She'd be a fool to entertain any kind of happily-ever-after ideas where Henry was concerned. He was right in that they were forever bound because of the boys, but the ties that bound them would be dual parenting and nothing more.

When the phone rang Henry went to answer, leaving Mary and Melissa alone. Melissa looked at the woman who had been so kind to her.

"I can't imagine what you must think of me," she said.

Mary smiled. "I certainly wouldn't want anyone to look at some of the things I've done in my life and make a judgment. I'm not about to do that to you."

"I appreciate that," Melissa replied gratefully.

As Melissa thought about all the ways coming here could have been so terrible, she was even more grateful to Mary and to Henry for their welcome, for embracing the boys and her into their home.

As Henry came back into the room James exploded in one of his rich belly laughs. Henry froze, the look on his face one of sheer wonder and delight.

"What's so funny, little man?" he asked as he leaned down and picked up the rattle James had dropped. He handed the rattle back to James, and James promptly threw it on the floor once again and looked at Henry and laughed. Henry laughed as well and picked up the rattle and once again gave it to James, who tossed it over the edge of the high chair tray yet again.

Melissa laughed. "That's his new game and he'll play as long as you will."

Henry's eyes sparkled with a new warmth she hadn't seen there before. "They're amazing, aren't they? It's obvious already that they're smart."

Melissa smiled. It was fun to see him being a proud daddy, certain that his boys were more intelligent and cuter than any other babies on the face of the earth.

The rest of the evening passed quickly. They drank hot cocoa and strung the popcorn and cranberry

garlands on the tree, then added tinsel and ornaments
that had been in the Randolf family for years.

Mary knew the history of each and every ornament
and Melissa was entranced by the stories she told.

"I picked these up while I was out today," Mary said
as she grabbed a box from the bookcase that Melissa
hadn't noticed. She took the lid off the box and pulled
out two ornaments and handed them to Melissa.

The ornaments were little cowboys and each sported
the words *Baby's First Christmas*. For a moment as
Melissa gazed at them her heart was too full to attempt
speech. "I don't know what to say," she finally managed
to sputter. A sudden mist fell in front of her eyes. She
quickly blinked them away. "Once again, thank you for
your kindness."

"Pick a good spot and hang them on the tree," Mary
said. "It's the beginning of a new tradition. There will
be an ornament every year for each of the boys to add
to the collection. When they leave home and have their
own trees, they can take them with them."

Melissa got up from the sofa and approached the tree,
vividly aware of Henry's eyes on her. She'd felt him
watching her all evening long, an intense, almost preda-
tory gaze that had kept her in a state of anticipation.

It was still there between them, that crazy, wild attraction, that white-hot desire that had exploded out of control
on the night of the snowstorm. She saw it in the depths of
his eyes, felt the electricity in the air whenever he was near.

She hung the ornaments and then James began to fuss.

"It's past their bedtime," she said as she unbuckled James from his high chair and pulled him up into his arms.

"I'll get this one," Henry said and picked up Joey.

"I think I'm going to call it a night as well," Melissa said to Mary. "Thank you for a wonderful evening and I'll see you in the morning."

Mary kissed each of the boys on their foreheads and smiled at Melissa. "Sleep well, Melissa."

As Melissa went up the stairs she was conscious of Henry just behind her. She could smell the scent of him, felt a stir in the pit of her stomach. It was easier to be around him with Mary in the room. Being alone with him made her think of how his lips had felt on hers, how his eyes had burned electric blue as he'd taken her that cold, wintry night.

She carried James into the bedroom across from where she'd slept the night before, where the two new cribs awaited. The boys were already dressed in their sleepers, but each needed a diaper change before going to sleep.

"You can just put him in that bed," she said. "And I'll take it from here."

"What else needs to be done?" he asked.

She smiled and unsnapped James's sleeper bottom. "Diaper duty."

"Toss me one of those diapers and I'll take care of Joey," he replied. She looked at him in surprise. "I wrestle cattle. I think I can handle wrestling a diaper on a little bottom," he said with a smile.

Within minutes the boys were changed and half-asleep. Melissa kissed their downy heads then walked to the doorway and turned out the light. A night-light glowed from a socket in the corner as she and Henry stepped back out into the hallway.

"That's it? Now they'll just go to sleep?" Henry asked.

"If we're lucky. If it's a good night," she replied.

"And if it's a bad night?"

He stood so close to her she could feel the heat from his body radiating to her. Memories of the night they'd shared shot through her mind. She remembered the feel of his hand around hers as they'd raced through the blinding snow to the abandoned farmhouse, his gentleness as he helped her pull off her wet shoes and socks.

He'd rubbed her feet between his hands, then had gotten a roaring fire started using a stack of wood that had been left by the fireplace.

As crazy as it sounded, that night in the arms of a stranger she'd felt more loved, more cared for than she'd ever felt in her life. It was a pathetic statement on how lonely her life had been up until now. She suddenly realized that even with Tom she had felt lonely.

She also realized he was looking at her expectantly, that he'd asked her a question she hadn't yet answered.

"If it's a bad night then I usually walk them or rock them until they finally go to sleep," she said. "Hopefully they won't have a bad night while we're here so they won't wake up you or your mother."

"You don't have to worry about them waking up Mom. Her rooms are on the other side of the house. And

I don't mind if they wake me up. I'd be happy to walk or rock a baby back to sleep."

She was quickly developing a crush on her babies' daddy and she found it appalling. "Then I guess I'll just say good-night," she said as she backed away from him.

"Good night, Melissa," he replied then turned his attention back to the bedroom where the boys slept.

It wasn't until Melissa was in her nightgown and had slid beneath the blankets on the bed that the first stir of uneasiness filtered through her.

The new cribs, the high chairs, even the ornaments on the tree suddenly took on an ominous meaning. She'd worried that Henry wouldn't want to be a part of Joey and James's lives but now her worry was exactly the opposite.

What if those things hadn't been bought to make her visit more pleasant? What if they'd been bought as the beginning to creating a permanent place here for the boys?

Henry certainly had the money and the power to make a play for custody of the boys and Melissa was in no financial position to be able to fight him.

Don't jump to conclusions, she told herself, but she couldn't stop the burning fear that somehow, someway, Henry intended to take her babies away from her.

Chapter 5

"Are we ready to take off?" Henry asked Melissa the next morning when they'd all finished breakfast. She looked so pretty in a bright pink sweater and worn jeans that hugged her hips, but she'd been unusually quiet since she'd gotten up that morning.

She glanced at the boys still seated in their high chairs. "Go on, Melissa. I can take it from here," Mary assured her. "Go enjoy a little shopping or whatever. It's a beautiful day and we won't see many more of them."

"I just need to get my coat," Melissa said.

As she ran up the stairs, Henry walked to the entry hall and retrieved his gun and shoulder holster from the drawer. He quickly put them on and then pulled on his winter coat.

He didn't want the presence of the gun to frighten Melissa, but he also didn't intend to go out the door without it. Although he anticipated no trouble, he intended to be prepared if trouble found him.

As she came back down the stairs he felt a tiny fluttering heat in the pit of his stomach. He was looking forward to spending some time with her, without the boys, without his mother as a buffer between them.

She intrigued him. He couldn't get a handle on her. He didn't know if she was really what she seemed—a nice woman who had acted uncharacteristically the night she'd been with him, a loving mother who had come here to find a friend, or a schemer who was like so many of the other women who had drifted through Henry's life.

"Ready," she said as she reached the landing.

He'd already had Charlie bring his truck to the driveway and as he stepped out the door he was on alert. As Charlie got out of the driver seat, Henry helped Melissa into the passenger side.

Once she was in he met Charlie at the driver door. "Thanks, Charlie," he said.

"No problem. You watch your back in town."

Henry nodded. "I'm sure we'll be fine. You keep an eye on things here while I'm gone. Oh, and Charlie, tell Hank I'm giving him three weeks' severance pay, but he's fired. I warned him about his drinking, but he didn't take my warning to heart."

Charlie's expression didn't change. "I'll tell him, boss."

Within minutes Henry was in the truck and they were pulling out of the ranch entrance and onto the main highway that led into Dalhart.

He cast her a sideways glance. "You've been rather quiet this morning."

She looked out the side window, making it impossible for him to see her face. "I was up most of the night. The boys were restless and fussy." She paused a moment and then continued, "You know it's not all fun and games, dealing with the boys. You've seen them on their best behavior, but they can be so difficult. They cry and fuss and keep you up all night. They spit out their food and make a big mess."

He frowned, wondering where she was going, what had brought on this little diatribe. "I'm aware that parenting isn't all fun and games," he replied.

She turned to look at him. "How could you possibly be aware of that? You've only been around them for a day and a half." Her eyes were wide and her lower lip trembled slightly.

"Only a fool thinks it's easy to raise kids, and I'm not a fool," he replied.

Once again she cast her gaze out the side window. She appeared at ease, but he could feel the tension wafting from her. Something had put a burr on her butt and he couldn't imagine what had caused it. Maybe she was just one of those moody women who got mad at the world without any provocation. Maybe this was a negative character trait that he would have seen if they'd dated for any length of time.

He figured eventually he'd know what had set her off. "Are you warm enough?" he asked as he turned the heater fan up a notch.

"I'm fine," she replied. She turned her head and he felt her steady gaze on him.

They rode in silence for only a few moments, then she sighed, an audible release that sounded weary. "You're obviously a man who is accustomed to getting what you want in life."

"I do all right," he replied cautiously. They had entered the town and he pulled into a parking space in front of Nathan's General Store. He unbuckled his seat belt and turned to look at his passenger. "Melissa, something is obviously bothering you. You want to tell me what's going on?"

Her eyes were filled with anxiety as she studied him. She raised a hand that trembled slightly to shove a strand of her long, pale hair behind her ear. "You scare me, Henry. Your power and your money scares me."

He looked at her in surprise. "It's been my experience that most women find my power and my money exciting—even intoxicating."

"Then I'm not most women," she replied. "Maybe those women had nothing to lose, but I do." Her voice thickened. "I need to know if you intend to take the boys away from me."

"What makes you think I'd do that?" he countered.

"Because you can," she replied and her eyes flashed with a touch of anger. "Because it's obvious you've already taken them into your life. You've bought cribs and high chairs and heaven knows what else and don't tell me you bought those things in order to make my visit with you more pleasant."

"I have no intention of taking the boys away from you," he said.

For a long moment their gazes remained locked. He saw the internal battle going on in her eyes, knew she was trying to decide if she could trust him or not.

"Melissa, I'm not going to lie to you. I want those boys living at the ranch. I want them to grow up here. I don't want to just be a weekend dad. I want to teach them to love the land, to be a part of Randolf Enterprises, which will one day be their legacy."

Her eyes narrowed with each of his words and he watched her stiffen in protest. She was a mother bear, sensing danger to her cubs and he liked that she looked as if she were about to rake his eyes out.

"I have a suggestion so that the boys will remain with you, but I also get what I want," he said.

"And what suggestion is that?" she asked dubiously.

"There's a carriage house behind the main house. It's a two-bedroom fully functional unit. I'd like you to consider moving there with the boys."

"That's a crazy idea," she said immediately. "I have a life in Amarillo."

He raised an eyebrow. "A full life? From what little you've told me, it sounds like a lonely life."

"But it's mine," she replied fervently. "It's my life, not yours."

Henry stifled a sigh of frustration. She'd said she was stubborn and at the moment that stubbornness lifted her chin and flashed in her eyes. "Look, I'd just like you to consider making the move. It would be great for the boys to have not just me, but my mother in their lives on a full-time basis. Just think about it. That's all I'm asking of you."

Once again those beautiful eyes of hers studied him thoughtfully. "And you promise that you won't try to take the boys from me. You won't use your money to try to get custody of them from me?"

"I promise," he replied.

"How do I know you aren't lying?"

He opened his truck door. "I guess you're just going to have to trust me, just like I'm trusting that the story you told me about some mystery woman bringing you to my house is true. Now, let's do a little shopping and let me show you the charms of Dalhart."

In all honesty, he hadn't really seriously considered going to court to take the boys away from her. They were babies, not some company he could buy or sell.

Besides, he knew how important a mother was to children. He had a wonderful relationship with his own mother and would never deprive his children in that way. He hoped Melissa could put away her fears at least for the duration of their outing and she appeared to as she got out of the truck and offered him a tentative smile.

"I'd like to pick up something for your mother while we're out," she said.

"You don't have to do that," he protested. He knew that money was tight for her.

"It's something I want to do," she replied, her chin once again lifted in that stubborn thrust. "She always smells like roses so I was thinking maybe some rose-scented soap or lotion."

He was surprised both by her observation about his mother and by her thoughtfulness. "Okay, I'm sure we can find something like that in one of the stores. I've got some things to pick up, too."

He gestured her toward the door of the store. Shopping at Nathan's General Store was kind of like delving into a treasure hunt.

The floor-to-ceiling shelves were stuffed full of items with no rhyme or reason for their placement there. Candles sat next to disposable diapers, jars of peanut butter next to boxes of cereal.

"Wow," Melissa exclaimed as they entered the store. "It looks like you could find whatever you need in this one store."

"If you can find what you need," Henry said dryly. "Nathan has an unusual way of arranging things."

"I can see that," she replied. "But that's just going to

make this fun." As she drifted toward a shelf, he watched her and wondered what it was that so drew him to her.

Granted, she was pretty, but it wasn't the heart-stopping beauty that could make a man yearn. She was pretty in a girl-next-door kind of way. But she wasn't a girl. She was a woman with lush curves that he remembered intimately. She also had an intriguing aura of a combination of strength and vulnerability. Certainly she had to be strong to take on the job of raising twins alone. But there were times when he saw a wistfulness in her eyes, a yearning for something that he had an idea had nothing to do with his money or his lifestyle.

A blue sweater, he thought suddenly. That's what she needed. A sweater the exact color of her eyes. He'd like to buy her several things, but he wasn't sure if his gifts would please her or make her angry.

He'd like to buy her a new robe to replace the one she'd been wearing yesterday morning. He'd like to buy her a new car to replace the junk on wheels that she'd driven to his house. But besides her strength and stubbornness he sensed more than a little bit of pride.

He liked that about her and yet knew it was that very trait that might make it difficult for him to get what he wanted.

Although he wouldn't mind another night of pleasure with her, he certainly didn't want to marry her. He didn't even want a romantic relationship with her. All he had to figure out was a way to convince her that it was in everyone's best interest for her to move into the carriage house. That's what he wanted more than anything and he would stop at nothing to get what he wanted.

Despite the anxiety that had weighed heavy in Melissa's heart from the moment she'd opened her eyes that morning, she was enjoying the unexpected shopping time with Henry. The talk in the truck had helped ease some of her fear. He'd promised he wouldn't try to take custody of the boys and she only hoped that she could trust that promise. She'd steadfastly refused to think about his offer of the carriage house. She might think about it later, but she didn't want her ambivalence to ruin a perfectly good day out.

They'd wandered in and out of stores and she'd been successful in buying rose-scented lotion and body soap for Mary.

Dalhart was a charming little city that Henry explained got an influx of tourists each summer.

In August there was a three-day celebration that included the largest free barbecue in the United States, a rodeo and three nights of live music and fun.

"See that building over there?" He pointed to a four-story brick structure on the corner. "That's the Randolf Hotel. I bought it six months ago and it is currently undergoing massive renovations. I'm going to need an interior designer when the renovations are done. I'd hire you if you were living here."

"Sounds suspiciously like a bribe," she replied lightly.

He grinned. "Maybe a little one. But I have to hire somebody and it might as well be you."

"You don't even know if I'm good at it," she exclaimed.

"I have a feeling you're good at whatever you put your mind to," he replied.

As they continued to walk the sidewalks Henry pointed out other places of interest and eventually led her to a café where he insisted they go inside and have a cup of coffee before heading back to the ranch.

She agreed. Although she was eager to get back to the kids, she was also reluctant for this time with Henry to end. He'd been charming, making her laugh with a surprising sense of humor and making her feel as if she were the most important person on the face of the earth.

He'd introduced her to people that greeted them and she'd seen the respect, the genuine admiration Henry's friends and neighbors had for him.

In the café they were led to a table in the back where they sat and ordered coffee. "I thought you said you had things to buy," she said once the waitress had poured their coffee and departed from the table.

"I got them," he replied.

"But you don't have any packages." She reached for the sugar to add to her coffee.

"I always have my purchases delivered to the house."

"I guess that's one of the perks about being you," she said dryly.

He grinned and the charm in that gesture kicked her in the heart. "I'm not going to lie. There are definitely perks to being wealthy. For instance, I never go to bed at night and worry about how I'm going to pay the rent. You'd have that same luxury if you'd move into the carriage house."

"That's not true. I would never expect to live someplace free of charge. I pay my way, Henry." She wrapped her hands around her coffee mug. It was one thing to be independent, but it was another to make the boys suffer from her independence.

"There are two things I'd ask of you," she said after a moment of hesitation.

"What's that?"

She realized this close that his eyes were really more gray than blue. Almost silver, they were the kind of eyes a woman could fall into, eyes a woman could lose herself in.

"I haven't been able to afford to get them health insurance," she said. "Maybe it would be nice if you could put them on your policy."

"Done," he answered without hesitation.

"The other thing is that maybe you could help me with a college fund for them. I didn't have the opportunity to go to college, but I'd like my sons to."

"You didn't have to ask for that. I'd want to make sure they go to college," he replied. "Why didn't you go?"

"There were several reasons. Financially it was impossible, but even with a full scholarship I couldn't have gone." She paused to take a sip of her coffee and then continued. "When I was a junior in high school my mother developed health complications due to diabetes. She lost most of her eyesight and they had to take one of her legs. There was no way I could leave her to go to college. She had nobody but me to take care of her."

"Quite a sacrifice on your part," he observed.

Melissa smiled. "I never considered it a sacrifice. I considered it a privilege to take care of the woman who had always taken care of me."

"One of the reasons I broke up with the woman I'd been dating for a while was because she thought it was time to put my mother into a nursing home."

Melissa looked at him in stunned surprise. "What was she thinking? Your mother certainly doesn't belong in a nursing home."

"My sentiments, exactly," he replied. "And you don't even need me to tell you what Mom thought of the idea. Needless to say Mom wasn't upset when I broke it off with Hilary. Now, tell me how you got involved with interior decorating."

As Melissa told him about working in a furniture store and finding her calling in arranging rooms and décor, she once again remembered the thrill of his mouth on hers, the way his arms had felt holding her tight.

"Shouldn't we be getting home?" she asked when she'd finished telling him about her struggling business. "It's been a couple of hours and I don't want to take advantage of your mother."

"We'll head back," he agreed. "But I can promise you

my mother wouldn't feel taken advantage of if we were gone all day. She's absolutely crazy over those boys."

Melissa smiled. "I can't tell you how wonderful it is that the boys not only have a father like you, but also a grandmother like Mary. I'm well aware of the fact that James the cowboy could have been a man who wanted nothing to do with them."

He looked at her sheepishly. "I want you to know that night was the first and only time I've lied about my name." He motioned for the waitress to bring their tab. "To be honest, that night I just wanted to be James the cowboy, not Henry Randolf III."

The café had grown busy with the approach of the noon hour and Melissa was aware of several people looking at her with curiosity as she and Henry left their table and headed for the door.

They were just about to reach the door when a tall, willowy brunette walked in. "Henry!" she cried in obvious delight, then her gaze swept to Melissa and her smile faltered slightly.

"Hilary, this is Melissa Monroe, a friend visiting from Amarillo. Melissa, this is Hilary Grant," Henry said.

"Nice to meet you," Hilary said to Melissa, then turned her attention back to Henry. "I was going to stop by your place this evening. I made a batch of that fudge you love and was going to bring it to you."

"That's not necessary," Henry protested.

"Well, of course it isn't necessary, but it's something I want to do. Will you be home this evening?"

"We'll be home, but it's Christmas Eve. It's really not a good time," he replied.

Her lush red lips pursed with a hint of irritation. "Then I'll give the fudge to Charlie to give to you tomorrow," she said. "I made it especially for you, Henry."

He smiled at the beautiful Hilary. "That was very nice, Hilary, and now we'd better get out of here. We're blocking the entrance."

"Nice to meet you, Hilary," Melissa said.

She nodded and returned Melissa's smile but there was nothing warm or inviting in the dark centers of her eyes. She swept past them toward a table where another woman sat as Melissa and Henry stepped out into the cold late morning air.

"Hilary knows Charlie?" Melissa asked.

"They're brother and sister," Henry replied.

She glanced up at him. "That must have been a bit awkward when you broke up with her."

"Actually, it was fine. Charlie doesn't seem to get involved with his sister's life. I get the feeling that they aren't real close."

They had gone only a few steps down the sidewalk when they came face-to-face with a short, squat man. Melissa felt Henry's instant tension. "Tom," he said and gave the man a curt nod.

"Henry. Heard you had some excitement out at your place the other night."

"And you wouldn't know anything about that,"

Henry replied. His eyes were cool, steely in a way Melissa hadn't seen before.

"Just what I hear through the grapevine. Sounds like there are some folks who aren't too happy about your decision to run for mayor."

"Just a handful, mostly the people who have something to lose if I get into office. You wouldn't be one of those people, would you, Tom?"

"Taking potshots at a man with a rifle isn't my style. You'll see me coming if I come after you." Tom gave Melissa a curt nod, then stepped around them and walked by.

"Who was that?" Melissa asked as they arrived at Henry's truck.

"Tom Burke, city manager and the man who definitely doesn't want me to become mayor." Henry opened her car door and she slid in and watched as he walked around the front of his truck to get into the driver side.

She could tell he was irritated. A muscle ticked in his strong jaw and his shoulders looked more rigid than usual.

"You don't like Tom Burke?" she asked as he got into the car.

"I think he's a criminal masquerading as an upstanding citizen," Henry replied as he started the truck. "He knows that if I get into office I'm going to do everything in my power to see that he loses his job."

"So, you think he's behind the attacks on you?"

He backed out of the parking space before replying. When he was on the road that led back to the ranch he visibly relaxed. "Yeah, Tom Burke is definitely at the top of my list of suspects. He knows I believe that he's been taking kickbacks from inferior contractors doing work for the city and he knows that if I succeed in being elected, his days are numbered."

"Have you told the sheriff this?"

He nodded, his dark hair gleaming in the sunshine that danced into the truck window. "Jimmy knows. Unfortunately Tom isn't the only councilman who I think is on the take. The corruption in this town runs deep and I'm determined to do some housecleaning."

"And what do the townspeople think?"

"I think they're behind me, but nobody has been brave enough to speak up. I'm hoping they'll speak by voting for me."

Melissa admired what he wanted to do. Like an old Wild West hero he was riding into town filled with outlaws with the intention of cleaning it up.

"She's very beautiful," she said.

He didn't pretend not to know who she was talking about. "She's okay."

She'd been more than okay, Melissa thought. Hilary Grant was stunning. Tall and slender, with lush long dark hair and exotic olive eyes, she'd looked like a model in her long, fashionable coat and boots.

"What does she do?" she asked curiously.

"She's a beautician and she does some local modeling gigs. She and Charlie had a pretty rough life and mostly Hilary is looking for somebody to change all that rather than figuring out how she can change it herself."

"She's in love with you, you know," she said.

"She was never in love with me," he scoffed. "She was always in love with my money."

"Were you in love with her?" Melissa was surprised to realize that his answer mattered. It mattered much more than it should to her.

"No, but there was a weak moment when I considered marrying her."

"You'd marry somebody you weren't in love with?" Melissa asked with surprise.

"I considered it a business deal," he replied with an easiness that astounded her. "Hilary would have made a good wife when it came to giving parties and acting as hostess for social affairs. In return she would have been able to live the lifestyle she desperately wants."

"And you'd do that? You'd marry as a business arrangement instead of for love?" Melissa asked.

"As far as I'm concerned love is overrated." He cast her a wry look. "I suppose you're one of those hopeless romantics?"

"Absolutely," she exclaimed. "I'll only marry for love. I want to marry somebody who loves me mindlessly, desperately, and I want to love him the same way. I want somebody to laugh with, to love, somebody to grow old with and love through eternity. And I won't settle for less."

As if to punctuate her sentence there was a loud pop. The truck careened wildly to the right side of the highway as Henry muttered a curse.

Melissa saw the deep ditch in front of them and knew they were going to hit it—hard. She squeezed her eyes closed and screamed as she felt the truck go airborne.

Chapter 6

Henry fought the steering wheel hard, trying to keep the truck on the road, but he lost the battle as the vehicle flew far right, hit the lip of the ditch and flew with all four tires off the ground. It came down with a crunch and a hiss, jarring the teeth in his head as it finally came to rest.

His heart raced and he quickly looked at Melissa. "Are you all right?"

She opened her eyes and gave a slow nod, but her face was chalky pale. "I'm okay." She drew in a deep breath and her hand shook as she shoved her hair away from her face. "I hope you have a spare," she said.

He pulled his gun from his holster with one hand and

reached for his cell phone with the other. Melissa's eyes widened at the sight of his weapon. But he didn't have time to deal with her fear.

He handed her the cell phone. "Call Jimmy." He rattled off Jimmy's cell phone number. "Tell him we're three miles from my place on the highway and somebody just shot out my tire."

As she made the phone call, Henry kept his gaze on the wooded area on the right side of the highway. He was ninety-nine percent certain that a mere second before the tire had blown he'd heard the unmistakable faint crack of a rifle.

"Jimmy said he's on his way," she said, her voice higher than normal in tone.

He felt her fear radiating across the seat, but he didn't look at her. Instead he kept focused on the area where he thought danger might come. He didn't know now if the attack was over or if the blown tire was just the beginning. Was somebody approaching the truck now, knowing it was disabled and that he and Melissa were sitting ducks?

Minutes ticked by—tense minutes of silence. He was grateful that Melissa understood his need for focus, for complete concentration, and didn't attempt to engage him in any way.

His heart continued to bang unusually fast, but as the fear began to recede, anger took its place. Who was behind these attacks? Dammit, there had to be something he and Jimmy could do to figure out who was responsible and get them behind bars.

Henry didn't relax until he saw Jimmy's patrol car pull up on the side of the road. Henry lowered his gun and opened his window as Jimmy got out of his car, gun drawn and headed across the ditch toward them.

"You're becoming a full-time job, Henry," Jimmy said as he reached the driver side of the truck. "You both okay?" He bent down to look at Melissa. "Ma'am?"

"I'm fine," she replied, her voice a little stronger than it had been moments before.

"You sure the tire was shot out?"

"I heard a crack right before the tire blew. I think it was a rifle shot."

Jimmy scanned the area. "You have any idea where the shot came from?"

"Somewhere in those trees, about a quarter of a mile back," Henry replied. "I'm sure whoever it was is gone now. If the intention was to do more harm, then he would have come after us while we were sitting here waiting for you."

"Any ideas on who might have taken the shot?" Jimmy asked.

"The usual suspects," Henry replied dryly. "Oh, and I have a new one to add. I fired Hank Carroll this morning before we left for town. You might want to check him out. Can you get somebody out here to take us home?"

Jimmy nodded. "I'll radio for Gordon to come out and give you a ride. Meanwhile I'll check out the woods and see if I find anything. You armed?"

Henry showed his gun. "Nobody is going to sneak

up on us. You see what you can find and we'll wait here for Gordon."

Jimmy nodded, hitched up his pants, then turned to walk back to his patrol car.

Henry shot Melissa a quick glance, pleased to see some of the color had returned to her cheeks. "I don't think we're in any danger," he said softly. "And I appreciate the fact that you haven't fallen into hysterics."

She offered him a faint smile, although her lips trembled slightly. "I'm really not the hysterical kind of woman. You fired Hank?"

He nodded and returned his gaze to the outside. "I'd warned him twice about drinking on the job, but he was half-lit when he carried in the tree yesterday."

"I noticed," she replied. "Would he do something like this?"

Henry frowned thoughtfully. "To tell the truth, I don't know. He hasn't been working for me very long. I hope this doesn't change your mind about living in the carriage house."

"I haven't made up my mind about living in the carriage house," she replied. "And I'd say now is definitely not a good time to ask me how I feel about living here."

At that moment a deputy car pulled up and Gordon Hunter got out. Jimmy returned as Henry and Melissa were getting into the backseat of Gordon's car.

"I couldn't find anything. I don't suppose you'd do me a favor and stay inside that secure castle of yours until I can figure out who's after you? I mean, tomorrow is Christmas, surely you don't have to be out anywhere."

"I won't be out and about for the next couple of days, but, Jimmy, I'm not going to become a prisoner in my own home," Henry replied.

Jimmy frowned. "I know, Henry. I'm doing the best I can but these drive-by shootings, so to speak, aren't giving me much to work with."

Henry clapped his hand on Jimmy's shoulder. He knew Jimmy was as frustrated as he was by these sneak attacks. He also knew Jimmy was a good man who took his job seriously.

"I'll arrange for Willie at the garage to pick up your car," Jimmy said. "And I'll be in touch in the next day or two. In the meantime, try to have a merry Christmas."

Henry nodded and got into the back of Gordon's car next to Melissa. "Okay?" he asked her.

"Never a dull moment with you, is there?" she said.

There was still a tiny flicker of fear still in the depths of her eyes and he reached over and took one of her hands in his. She immediately curled her cold fingers with his as if she'd desperately needed the contact with him.

He was surprised by the sudden surge of protectiveness that filled him holding her small, slender hand in his. He wanted to keep her from harm. Surely it was only because she was the mother of his children and nothing more.

Still, he was equally surprised to realize that he had no desire to release her hand until Gordon deposited them at the front door of his house.

Melissa grabbed her shopping bags and Henry ushered her into the house, where Mary met them at the door. "What happened?" she asked, worry thick in her voice.

"Nothing serious, just a blowout," Henry said quickly before Melissa could reply. "The spare was flat and Gordon just happened to be driving by so we hitched a ride home with him."

The last thing he wanted to do was worry his mother, but he wasn't sure if Melissa would play along with his story.

She did, not countering his story to his mother. "How were the boys?" Melissa asked. "Did they behave for you?"

Mary's face lit up. "They were absolute angels," Mary said as Henry flashed Melissa a grateful smile.

As Melissa and his mother disappeared into the house Henry headed for his office. He needed to call the garage about his truck and he needed to talk to Charlie to see how things had gone with Hank.

The main thing he needed was some distance from Melissa. Even with the concern that somebody had shot out his tire, he couldn't stop thinking about how nice her hand had felt in his, how the scent of her had dizzied his senses all morning long.

He wanted her. He wanted her naked in his arms, gasping beneath him as she'd been on the night they'd shared. But she'd made it clear what she was looking for—that happily-ever-after and love forevermore nonsense. That definitely wasn't what he'd be offering to her.

Would she be interested in a night of passion with him with no strings attached, no promise of love or commitment? It was possible.

He knew she wasn't immune to the sparks that snapped in the air between them. He'd seen an awareness in her eyes when he got too close to her, noticed the way her gaze lingered on him when she thought he wasn't looking.

He sank down at his desk and realized it was much easier to speculate on how to get Melissa into bed than trying to figure out who in the hell was trying to kill him.

"You're perfectly safe here," Henry said later that evening to Melissa. "The house has a state-of-the-art security system. Nobody can get in here without me knowing about it."

Melissa nodded and took a sip of her wine. Mary had just gone to bed, the boys were also down for the night, and Henry and Melissa were sitting in the living room with the glow of the Christmas tree lights the only illumination in the room.

There was no question that the safety of her sons had been on her mind all afternoon and evening. How could she even consider moving here knowing that somebody wanted to do harm to Henry? Knowing that it was possible she or her boys could be casualties in whatever war was being waged?

"I can't seriously consider moving here until the

issue is resolved, not that I'm seriously considering it anyway," she said, giving voice to her thoughts.

"But I want you to consider it seriously," Henry said. He paused to take a sip of his scotch. "The special election is in February. Certainly by then I'm confident that Jimmy will be able to figure out who is hassling me. It would probably take you that long to make the move anyway."

"Hassling you?" She raised one of her eyebrows at him. "Honestly, that's a pretty weak description for what's happened just since I've been here. That tire blowout could have killed us both. The truck could have rolled and we wouldn't be sitting here right now."

"I swear I won't do anything to put you or the boys in danger," he replied.

She shrugged. "It doesn't matter now. I plan on going home tomorrow afternoon."

"But it will be Christmas Day," he protested. "You can't leave tomorrow. You'll break Mom's heart."

She smiled at him. "Ah, first you try to bribe me with a job offer and now you're using your mother to manipulate me. You should be ashamed of yourself."

He laughed and that familiar warmth shot through her at the pleasant sound. "I refuse to feel guilty if it forces you to stay a little longer. Besides, Etta will be making a traditional Christmas feast for lunch tomorrow and what difference does another day or two make?"

"You just want more time to try to talk me into moving here," she said.

He nodded, his eyes teasing her. "There is that," he agreed.

"Okay, I won't leave tomorrow. But the next morning we've got to get back home."

He finished his scotch and set the glass down on the coffee table. "And what then?" The teasing light in his eyes vanished. "When will I see the boys again?"

Melissa realized that her life was about to get more complicated. She'd been thrilled that Henry wanted to be a part of the boys' lives, but now she was faced with the logistics of how they would make it all work.

"I guess I can commit to twice a month driving here for a weekend visit," she said. "I know it isn't ideal, that you'd like to see the twins every day," she added as she saw the dismay on his face. "But, Henry, you have to work with me here."

"I know." He leaned back against the sofa and frowned thoughtfully. "I never knew how kids would make me feel, how much they'd make me want to be there for them, to protect them and teach them. I never dreamed that thoughts of them would be so all-consuming."

She smiled, finding him even more attractive than ever with love for his children—for her children—shining from his eyes. "Welcome to parenthood."

He shook his head and smiled. "I never knew it would be like this." His features were soft in the glow from the Christmas lights and Melissa found herself wishing for things that could never be.

She wished she and Henry were married and

tonight after checking on their children they'd get into bed together and make love all night long. She wished they'd share breakfast the next morning and talk about their shared dreams, laugh over secret jokes and know that they would face each other over their first cup of coffee every morning for the rest of their lives.

Foolish wishes, she knew. Wishes brought on by the glow of the Christmas tree and the warmth of family that permeated this house. She was slowly being seduced by Henry and his mother and she knew she'd be a fool to hope for anything except weekend visits for the boys and nothing more.

Still, she'd allowed him to talk her into staying another day because she'd been reluctant to leave this house of warmth, reluctant to leave him.

"Are there twins in your family?" he asked, pulling her from her wayward thoughts.

"Not that I know of. What about yours?"

"I think there were twins on my father's side of the family," he replied.

The doorbell rang and Henry checked his watch with a frown. "Who could that be?" Melissa watched as he rose from the sofa with a masculine grace.

When he disappeared from her sight, she leaned back in her chair and released a sigh. She'd enjoyed the day with him far too much.

His ideas about marriage had shocked her. Was he so afraid a woman would take his money? Did he not believe that he was worth anything simply as a man? What good was it to have money if all it made you do was worry about who might take it away from you?

She wondered what had made Henry so cynical about love. Had some woman hurt him in the past? Certainly Tom had hurt her, but even the pain of his rejection hadn't made her belief in true love waver.

When he returned he carried his car keys with him. "That was Willie from the garage. He delivered my truck." He pocketed the keys and sat back down on the sofa.

"Henry, do you have a computer?" she asked. She knew he had never really embraced her story about MysteryMom and more than anything she wanted him to believe that she had no interest in any of his money for herself.

"Sure, in my study. Why?"

"I was wondering if maybe you could let me use it to see if I can connect with MysteryMom. This is the time of the evening when I normally could find her in the chat room. It's important to me that you believe what it was that brought me here to you."

"You haven't given me a reason not to believe you."

She heard the faint edge of doubt in his voice and the *yet* that had remained unspoken. What he meant was that she hadn't given him a reason not to believe her *yet*.

"Maybe not, but for my own peace of mind I'd like to show you."

Once again he got up from the sofa. She finished her wine and then followed him down the hallway to the study. The room had seemed enormous the first time she'd been in here, but as he gestured her into the chair behind the desk and he stood immediately behind her, the room seemed to shrink.

They waited for the computer to boot up, and she was intensely aware of his scent, that provocative scent of clean male and spicy cologne. She could feel his warm breath on the nape of her neck and she fought a shiver of pleasure and hoped he didn't notice that she was suddenly breathless.

"There you go," he said. "You're Internet connected and can go wherever you want to go."

She placed her hand on the mouse and began to maneuver her way to the chat room where night after night for months she had talked to MysteryMom and other single mothers and mothers-to-be. But when she tried to find the room where she had spent so much of her time, bared so much of her soul, it was gone.

"I don't understand," she muttered softly as she clicked and whirled the mouse in an effort to locate the chat room. "It's not here." She felt a sick frustration welling up inside her.

"Melissa, it's Christmas Eve, that's probably why nobody is there." He placed his hand on her shoulder.

"No, you don't understand. The room always had a virtual sign welcoming single mothers and it's gone. The room itself isn't there anymore."

She looked up at him, surprised to feel thick emotion rising up inside her. She'd wanted to prove to him that it had been MysteryMom who had brought her here and not his money or the lure of a life on easy street.

"Do you have an e-mail address for this Mystery-Mom?"

She shook her head negatively. "We always just talked in the room. If we wanted to talk privately we instant messaged each other. I only got one e-mail from her and that was the directions here, but when I tried to answer her back my reply bounced back to me." She covered his hand with one of hers. "You have to believe me, Henry. It's so important to me."

He gazed at her for a long moment. It was a piercing gaze, as if he were looking into her very soul. "I believe you, Melissa. You don't have to prove anything to me."

He pulled his hand from her shoulder and turned off the computer. "Come on, it's getting late and Santa will come early in the morning."

She was ready to get out of the study, ready to get away from him. His scent, the gentle touch of his hand and the way he'd gazed at her had all combined to make her feel more than a little weak in the knees.

They left the study and as they walked back through the living room Henry turned out the Christmas tree lights, then turned on a switch that illuminated the stairs. They climbed up the stairs side by side and again Melissa was struck with a wistfulness that things were different between her and Henry. Everything would have been much less complicated if they'd dated for a long time, fallen in love and then she'd gotten pregnant.

And if wishes were horses, I'd have a whole herd, she thought. When they reached the top of the stairs she went into the boys' room and Henry followed right behind her.

She went to Joey's crib first and her heart expanded in her chest as she saw him sleeping peacefully. He had a little smile on his lips, as if his dreams were happy.

She then checked on James, unsurprised to see that he'd managed to wiggle himself sideways in the crib and had worked the blanket off him. She didn't attempt to move him from his position, but covered him again with the blanket, then backed away from the crib and into the hallway.

"James is a restless sleeper. He's more easily awakened than Joey and never keeps his blankets on," she said softly as she moved across the hall to her bedroom doorway. "I guess then I'll just say good-night."

"Melissa, I enjoyed spending the morning with you." He took a step toward her and stood so close she could feel the radiating warmth of his body.

"I had a nice time with you, too," she replied as her heart drummed a little faster.

There was a heat in his eyes that excited her and when he reached up to smooth a strand of her hair back from her face his simple touch electrified her.

"I thought about you often after that night," he said, his voice a husky whisper that stirred a simmering fire inside her. "I wondered if you'd gotten where you were going okay, if somehow, someway, our paths would ever cross again. I can't believe how little we shared and yet how much we shared."

"It was a crazy night," she replied half-breathlessly.

"I'm feeling a little crazy right now." He didn't give her time to think, time to process what he'd just said. He pulled her into his arms and his lips claimed hers.

It never occurred to her to step back from him, to deny him and herself the pleasure of kissing him. Just as she remembered, his lips were a combination of tenderness and command, of controlled hunger.

She opened her mouth to allow him to deepen the kiss. His body was rock-hard against hers as his hands slid down her back and pulled her closer to him.

Their tongues swirled and danced and Melissa felt herself falling into a sensual haze of instant desire. No man had ever been able to stir her like Henry. No man had ever made her feel as alive as she felt in his arms, with his mouth on hers.

He released her suddenly and stepped back, his eyes hooded and dark. Melissa fought for composure when all she really wanted was to grab him by the arm and pull him into the bedroom with her. Then she was struck by a thought that dashed all desire away.

"You've tried bribery and manipulation to get me to agree to move here. Is seduction your next weapon to use?" she asked.

A slow grin curved the edges of his mouth upward. "I promise you I will never seduce you in order to get you to move into the carriage house. The only reason I would seduce you is strictly for my own personal pleasure and nothing more."

He reached out and touched her lower lip with his index finger. "And I do intend to seduce you, Melissa. But, for tonight, sleep well and I'll see you in the morning."

Chapter 7

Henry awakened the next morning with a sense of excitement he hadn't felt since he'd been a very young boy. The air smelled of Christmas, of baking cinnamon rolls and fresh evergreen boughs and the cranberry-scented candles his mother loved to burn.

For a moment he remained in bed, thinking about the day ahead and the night before. Kissing Melissa had been an early Christmas present to himself. He'd wanted to kiss her all day.

As he watched her wander through the stores, her lips pursed thoughtfully as she considered her purchases, all he could think about was capturing that lush mouth with his own. Even in those moments immediately after the blowout he'd wanted to cover her trembling mouth with his and kiss her until the fear in her eyes transformed to something else.

Kissing her had been just like he remembered. Her lips had been soft and hot and welcoming and he hadn't wanted to stop. He'd wanted to take her by the hand and lead her to his bed.

Afterward he'd told her good-night and he'd gone back downstairs and spent the next several hours wrapping presents and placing everything he'd bought and the items that had been delivered over the past twenty-four hours under the tree.

By the time he'd finished it looked like toy land had come to the Randolf home. As pleased as he was about what he'd bought the twins, he couldn't wait for Melissa to open her presents from him.

It had been a long time since Henry had been excited about giving to somebody else. Sure, he was a generous contributor to a variety of charities, but buying for Melissa had given him a special kind of pleasure.

He pulled himself from bed and after a shower left the master suite. It was just after six when he passed Melissa's door and glanced inside to see her still in bed.

She was nothing more than a short, lean lump beneath the blankets, her hair the only thing visible. He wanted to crawl beneath the blankets with her, pull her into his arms and make love to her as the sun crested the horizon. That would definitely make it a Christmas to remember.

Instead he backed away from the doorway and checked on the boys, who were still sleeping soundly. He drew in a deep breath of their baby scent and felt a piercing ache at the thought of having to tell them goodbye even for a brief time.

He continued down the stairs. The tree was lit up, candles burned on the mantel and two stockings were hung, each with one of the boy's names in big glittery letters. His mother had been busy already.

He found her in the dining room, sipping a cup of coffee. She stood as he entered and gave him a kiss on the cheek. "Merry Christmas, Henry," she said, her eyes twinkling as brightly as the lights on the tree.

He hugged her and returned the greeting. "You're up early," he said as he poured himself a cup of coffee from the silver coffeepot in the center of the table.

"I couldn't stay in bed another minute. I can't wait for Melissa to see everything we've bought for the boys. I can't wait to see them in the little outfits I bought for them." She smiled and shook her head. "Christmases are going to be wonderful from now on."

"When Melissa and I sit down to discuss the visitation, I'll insist that the twins are here at Christmastime," he replied, although the words certainly brought him no comfort.

He wanted the boys here all the time. He wanted to see their first steps, he wanted to hear the first time they said da-da. He didn't want to wait days or weeks at a time between visits.

"You haven't managed to talk her into moving here? Staying in the carriage house?" Mary asked.

"Not yet. But I still have until tomorrow to make my case," he replied.

"She's leaving tomorrow?" Mary's dismay showed on her features.

"That's what she says."

"It would be nice if we could talk her into staying until after New Year's Eve."

Henry grinned knowingly at his mother. "Then we could try to convince her to stay until after Valentine's Day, or maybe Easter."

Mary laughed and nodded. "I don't have a problem with that." Her smile grew thoughtful. "It's not just the boys. I like Melissa. She's the kind of girl I once dreamed that you'd marry and build a family with."

Henry scowled. "You know that's not happening so don't even start." Most of the time Mary seemed to respect his decision to remain single, but occasionally she launched a sneak attack in an attempt to get him to change his mind.

"If not Melissa, then surely you can find some nice woman to fall in love with," she continued as if he hadn't spoken. "I hate the idea of you growing old alone. I want you to have what your father and I shared."

He paused to take a sip of his coffee. "I have sons who will keep me company as I grow old and that's all I need."

"I'm just saying it would be nice if they all could be here full-time."

Henry leaned back in his chair. "I have a feeling she isn't going to make a decision about moving here until I can assure her that it's safe. The greeting committee of bullets flying has to play a role in her not even considering it right now."

"Jimmy still doesn't have any idea who is responsible?" she asked with concern.

Henry shook his head. "He's coming over tomorrow and we're going to sit down and discuss the whole thing."

At that moment Melissa appeared in the doorway, a twin on each hip. Both Mary and Henry jumped up to take the boys from her.

"Merry Christmas," she said, her eyes sparkling brightly. She looked beautiful in a cheerful red sweater and jeans. Her cheeks were flushed with color and her hair was shiny and smooth to her shoulders.

"And the same to you," Mary said as she took Joey from Melissa's arm.

Henry took James, who offered him a half-cranky smile, then fussed and kicked his feet. "They're hungry," Melissa said. "I'll just go make them some cereal and I'll be right back."

Henry watched her disappear while he put James into his high chair. The fussing stopped, as if James knew he was about to get what he wanted. Within seconds Mary had both boys giggling as she made funny faces and silly noises. The sound of their laughter welled up inside Henry, filling him with such love it brought unexpected tears to his eyes.

Sons.

His sons.

He still couldn't quite wrap his mind around it and he was thankful for the blizzard that had brought him and Melissa together for that single night that had resulted in Joey and James.

There was no way he wanted a long-distance relationship with them. What if Melissa tired of the drive back and forth from Amarillo to here? What if eventually she fell in love and married a man who resented sharing the boys?

Fear clutched his heart at the very thought. He had to convince Melissa to move into the carriage house. It was the only way Henry could get what he wanted—a full-time position in his sons' lives.

He smiled as she came back into the room carrying two cereal bowls. "You sit back and enjoy your coffee. Mom and I will do the honors," he said as he took the bowls from her. "Did you sleep well?"

"Like a log," she replied. She poured herself a cup of coffee and sat in the chair next to Henry. Instantly he could smell the scent of her, clean and floral and intoxicating.

"Etta should have breakfast ready in about fifteen minutes," Mary said as she spooned cereal into Joey's mouth. "And after that we'll go in and see what Santa left for us."

"Santa has already given me more than enough," Melissa said. Her eyes were filled with warmth as she looked first at Mary, then at him. "The welcome you've both given me is more than I ever expected to find this Christmas."

"Maybe later today you would let Henry show you the carriage house," Mary said, surprising Henry with her forwardness. "Just have a peek at it before you definitely make up your mind one way or the other."

"I guess I could do that," Melissa agreed slowly, but she lifted her chin in the gesture Henry had come to know as stubborn pride.

At that moment Etta entered the dining room carrying a tray of fist-size biscuits, a bowl of gravy and a platter of scrambled eggs.

Breakfast was pleasant with he and his mother telling tales of Christmases past and Melissa sharing some of her fond childhood memories of the holiday when her mother had been alive. Henry found his gaze drawn to her again and again. She looked so soft, so inviting and it was more than memories of the sex they'd shared that attracted him to her.

He loved the sound of her laughter. He liked the habit she had of shifting that shiny strand of hair behind her ears when she was thinking or when she was nervous.

He felt a little like he had in seventh grade when he'd had a crush on a girl named Angela. She'd been blond-haired and blue-eyed like Melissa and it had taken him months to work up his nerve to ask her to a school dance. The experience had been his first taste of how materialistic women, even very young women, could be.

He shoved the ancient painful memory away as he

focused on the conversation and the musical ring of Melissa's laughter.

When they were all finished eating they adjourned into the living room, where the first thing his mother insisted they do was dress the boys in the little Santa suits she'd bought for them.

As the women dressed the little ones, Henry moved the high chairs into the room, as excited as a kid to distribute the presents to everyone. When the boys were in their little Santa suits, Mary took dozens of pictures and Henry knew she'd be sporting those photos all around town, bragging about her grandbabies.

Henry donned a Santa hat that James found incredibly funny. As the little boy laughed that rich burst of joy, Henry knew this was definitely going to be a Christmas to remember.

Melissa sat on the sofa next to Mary as Henry began to unveil the bigger presents hidden under sheets. Rocking horses and walkers and stuffed animals as big as Henry himself were just the beginning. There were boxes of clothes and diapers and educational toys. Of course, the boys liked the shiny wrapping paper best of all.

Mary opened her gift of the lotion and soap from Melissa and exclaimed that it was the brand and scent that she loved.

Melissa was already feeling overwhelmed when Henry gave her a present. "You shouldn't have," she said to him.

He smiled. "Open it, Melissa. I picked it out just for you. It's the exact color of your eyes."

Melissa couldn't help the way her heart fluttered at his words. She carefully removed the wrapping paper and opened the box to display the most beautiful blue sweater she'd ever seen in her life. It was soft as a whisper and she was touched by his thoughtfulness.

"Oh, Henry. It's beautiful." She felt the ridiculous burn of tears at her eyes.

"That's not all." He handed her a larger package. "I hope you won't be offended by the more personal nature of this gift, but I couldn't resist it."

She frowned at him, wondering just how personal the gift might be, aware that his mother was seated right next to her. It was a robe, a beautiful long burgundy robe with a satin collar and belt. He must have noticed the worn condition of her robe.

One of the things she was grateful for was that although he had been extravagant with the things he'd bought for the boys, the things he'd bought for her had been ordinary presents, as if he'd known she'd be displeased if he went overboard for her.

"I have something for you, Henry." Melissa got up from the sofa and grabbed the small present she'd slipped under the tree when she'd come downstairs that morning. He looked at her in surprise, took the gift and sat in one of the chairs to open it.

"There's not much I can buy for a man who appears to have everything," Melissa said. "But I know it's something you don't have, something I think you'll want to have."

He looked at her curiously, then ripped the paper off to expose two small frames. Inside the frames were the newborn pictures of the boys and two cigars with bands that exclaimed, "It's a Boy."

His eyes filled with emotion as he gazed at the gifts, then back at her. "It's the most perfect present you could have given me." He stood and kissed her on the cheek. "Thank you."

Her skin burned with the press of his lips and once again she felt overwhelmed by the warmth, by the feel of family and by the gifts he and Mary had bought for her sons.

By ten o'clock most of the mess from the morning had been cleaned up and the doorbell rang to announce a guest. Henry went to answer as Melissa finished placing the last of the wrapping paper into a large garbage bag.

She tensed as she heard the familiar female voice. Hilary. The sharp pang of jealousy that roared through Melissa stunned her. She shouldn't feel jealous of any woman Henry might have in his life. She had no right to feel that kind of emotion.

As Hilary walked into the living room she stopped short at the sight of the twins in their chairs. She looked at the boys, then at Henry, and her pretty features tightened with stunned surprise.

"Hello, Hilary," Melissa said. The woman was exceptionally beautiful and sophisticated in a gold sweater and tight black slacks. Her dark hair was pulled up and gold earrings danced at her dainty ears. She carried in her hands a platter that Melissa assumed was the famous fudge she'd promised Henry the day before.

"Merry Christmas, Mary and Melinda," Hilary replied.

"Melissa. My name is Melissa."

"Of course," Hilary said, then turned her attention to Henry. "Could I speak to you privately for a moment?"

"Okay. Let's go into my study." Henry gestured her down the hallway.

"I can't imagine what he ever saw in that woman," Mary said the minute they had disappeared.

"She's very beautiful," Melissa said as she put the last of the wrapping paper into the trash.

"Maybe on the outside, but it's inner beauty that really matters. Now, if you'll excuse me, I'm going to go help Etta with the lunch preparations."

"And I'm going to put the boys down for their nap," Melissa replied.

Minutes later Melissa stood in the doorway of the room she now thought of as the nursery. Joey had fallen asleep almost immediately and James was almost there, fussing a bit as he fought sleep.

As he finally gave up the battle, Melissa turned from the door and gasped in surprise at the sight of Hilary in front of her.

"He won't marry you, you know," she said softly.

"I don't expect him to marry me," Melissa replied.

Hilary smiled. "He's not going to marry me, either. I'd hoped that eventually I could wear him down, but Henry has no interest in being married. You seem like a nice woman and it would be a shame for you to get hurt."

"I appreciate your concern, but trust me, Henry has made it clear to me a hundred different ways that he's not the marrying kind. Besides, what makes you think I would want to marry him?"

Hilary looked at her and released a dry laugh. "You're kidding, right? I mean, he's good-looking and nice and wealthy. Why wouldn't you want to marry him?"

Melissa couldn't believe she was having this conversation with a woman who had been Henry's lover. "My life is in Amarillo. I'll be going home tomorrow to my life."

"Well, in any case I just came up here to tell you that it was nice to meet you and I hope you have a safe trip home." With a curt nod, Hilary turned around and walked down the stairs.

Melissa drew a deep breath and went into her bedroom. While the morning had been one of the happiest she could ever remember, she felt a sudden burn of tears in her eyes.

There was no way she'd ever to be able to provide for the twins like Henry could. Would she be denying her sons by choosing not to move here? She didn't want to do the wrong thing, but she didn't know what was the right thing. Maybe she should just take a look at the carriage house and keep an open mind.

Still, she couldn't ignore the fact that somebody was trying to hurt Henry and it was possible she and the boys might become accidental victims.

"Melissa?"

She whirled around to see Henry standing in the doorway. "Everything all right?" he asked.

"Everything is fine," she replied.

"I know Hilary came up here. She didn't say anything to upset you, did she?" He gazed at her worriedly.

Melissa smiled. "Not at all. She simply told me that it was nice to meet me and she hoped I had a safe trip home."

He seemed relieved. "Hilary tends to have a bit of a sharp tongue."

"Don't worry, Henry. I'm a big girl and I can take care of myself."

He nodded. "I was wondering if while the twins are napping if now would be a good time to take you to see the carriage house." He smiled, that slow sexy grin that heated every ounce of blood in her body. "I was also wondering when I was going to get to see that blue sweater on you."

"Why don't you give me five minutes and I'll meet you downstairs and we can take a look."

"Great. I'll meet you downstairs."

The minute he left the room she closed the door and pulled the sweater out of the box. It fit perfectly and was exactly the color of her eyes. The fact that he'd even thought about her eyes made her heart flutter just a little bit.

It was only as she was walking down the stairs that she realized the terrible truth—she was more than a little bit in love with Henry Randolf III.

Chapter 8

The morning had gone far better than Henry had hoped. The living room had been filled with laughter, warmth and a feeling of family that had been missing from the house since his father's death.

Melissa had teased him as if they'd known each other forever, and in many ways that's the way he was beginning to feel about her. She was comfortable, and yet made him simmer with expectancy. He couldn't remember a woman who had done both for him.

He pulled on his holster and his gun and then covered it with his winter coat. Despite the fact that it was a holiday and the season of peace and joy, Henry couldn't let down his guard. He was eager to have a sit-down meeting with Jimmy the next day to see if the lawman had come up with any evidence as to who might be after him. They needed to come up with a plan to force the person out into the open.

He turned as Melissa came down the stairs, clad in the blue sweater and the jeans that did amazing things for her legs and curvy butt. Something about her stole his breath away.

Lust, he told himself. That was it. Lust and nothing more. If he slept with her again he was certain these crazy feelings would go away.

Her plans were to leave in the morning and short of locking her up in a tower, there was no way he could stop her. He pulled her coat from the closet and held it out to her. "Ready?"

She nodded. "Ready."

"I've got to say, you look sexy as hell in that sweater."

"I'll bet you say that to all the girls," she replied lightly but her cheeks flushed as she pulled on her coat.

They stepped out the door, and Henry threw an arm around her shoulder. He told himself it was because he wanted to protect her if somebody came at them, but the truth was he'd been dying to touch her all day.

She didn't pull away but instead snuggled into him as the cold wind whipped her hair against his face. They walked briskly, not speaking. Henry kept his gaze bouncing left and right, relaxing as he saw Charlie and several of his men in the distance.

When they reached the carriage house he unlocked

the door and ushered her into the foyer. "You might want to keep your coat on. We just have the minimal heat running in here right now."

She nodded, stepped into the living room and caught her breath. "Oh, my gosh. This is four times the size of my apartment."

It was an open floor plan, the living room flowing into the kitchen. The living-room flooring was a soft beige carpeting and the kitchen had an attractive tile in Southwest colors. The furnishings were simple but tasteful and the kitchen was fully equipped with every pot and pan that a chef might need.

"If you wanted to bring in your own furniture we could store all of this," he said, unable to read the expression on her face. "Let me show you the bedrooms." He led her down a short hallway to the first bedroom. It was definitely large enough to accommodate two cribs and later two twin beds for the boys. From the window the stables and corral were in view, perfect for two little cowboys.

From there he led her into the master bedroom, which was huge, with an adjoining bathroom complete with a Jacuzzi tub. For a moment his head filled with a vision of how she'd look in that tub with her shiny hair piled up on her head and her body surrounded by scented bubbles. He tried desperately to shove the provocative vision out of his mind.

She wandered around the room and when she finally turned to look at him, tears glimmered in her eyes. Instead of looking pleased, she looked achingly miserable.

"What's wrong?" he asked.

The tears spilled from her eyes onto her cheeks. "I don't know what to do. I'm so confused. I'm so overwhelmed by everything."

Henry realized at that moment he didn't like to see her cry. He walked over to her and captured her pretty face between his palms. The look in her eyes was slightly wild, as if she wanted to escape him and the entire situation.

"Melissa, don't cry," he said gently. "Tell me what's wrong."

She jerked away from him and took several steps backward. "You don't understand. This place is so wonderful and all the things you bought for the boys were unbelievable. I know they could have a wonderful life here, but they could have a wonderful life with me in Amarillo, too."

She raised her chin and swiped angrily at her tears. "Lots of children just see their father on the weekends and they survive just fine. People get divorced or never marry and visitation is worked out okay."

He stared at her for a long moment. "But that's not what I want," he said. He shoved his hands into his coat pockets and leaned against the wall. "I don't want to be a weekend dad. What can I do to make this work for you? Of course I'd take care of all your moving expenses and if you have a lease that needs to be broken, I'll take care of that, too. If you're worried about work, I'm sure I can find you some clients for your interior decorating and there's always the hotel that you could be contracted to do. I can take care of all your needs, Melissa. We can make this work."

As he'd spoken, her tears had dried and she gazed at him with an inscrutable expression. When he finished she shook her head and offered him a small, somehow sad smile.

"Henry, there are some things your money just can't buy. You can't buy me. I don't care about money or things. My mother and I didn't have money, but we were happy." She paused and frowned.

"So, this is a no?" he asked flatly.

"It's an I don't know," she replied with obvious frustration. "I've known you and your mother for a couple of days. I refuse to make a life-altering decision that quickly. What I suggest is that I go home tomorrow and think things through without your influence. I want to do what's best for everybody, Henry, and that includes what's best for me."

Although he was disappointed with her decision, he couldn't help but admire her strength in not succumbing to an easier life than the one he thought she was currently living.

"You know I won't stop trying to change your mind," he said lightly, hoping to dispel some of the tension that sparked in the air between them.

She offered him a smile. "Why am I not surprised by that?" She walked out of the bedroom and he followed just behind her.

"I told you I was stubborn," he said.

"Just be aware that you might have met your match," she replied.

As they stepped out of the carriage house he noticed that the sun had disappeared beneath a thick layer of clouds and the air felt colder than it had before.

What he needed was a good old-fashioned blizzard that would make Melissa stay long enough for him to get her to agree what he wanted.

But Henry knew there were two things he couldn't control. The weather was the first and apparently Melissa was the second.

It began to snow at nine o'clock that evening. Melissa stood at her bedroom window and stared out in dismay. If this kept up there was no way she could leave after breakfast in the morning like she'd planned.

She checked on the boys, who were sleeping soundly, then went back down the stairs where she knew Henry was probably having a glass of scotch. Funny, after such a brief time she'd begun to know his habits. He usually sat in the living room to unwind after his mother excused herself for bed.

Sure enough, he was seated in his chair, a glass of scotch at his side as he stared at the lights still twinkling on the Christmas tree. He smiled when she appeared in the doorway. "How about a glass of wine?"

"That sounds nice," she agreed and sat on the sofa while he went to the bar and poured her drink.

It was odd, anytime she was near him a sizzle of anticipation raced through her and yet she was also comfortable with him. He was an easy man to be around, easy to talk to and share things with.

As he handed her the glass of wine, she again wondered if somehow somebody had hurt him in the past. Had somebody made him believe that he had nothing to offer a woman except for his bank account and a lavish lifestyle? His money seemed to be the only bargaining chip he knew how to use to get the things he wanted in life.

"Looks like your plans to take off tomorrow morning might have to be postponed," he said as he returned to his chair.

"Don't look so smug about it," she replied teasingly. "Actually, I'm hoping it stops soon and the roads will be all right for travel by morning."

"And I'm hoping it snows until March and you're forced to stay here and I'll have all that time to convince you to move into the carriage house."

She laughed. "You're positively relentless." She took a sip of her wine and eyed him curiously. "Tell me why you're such a cynic when it comes to love. Haven't you ever been in love before?"

"The last time I was in love I was in seventh grade. Her name was Angela and I was absolutely crazy about her." He took a drink of his scotch and then continued. "It took me months to get up the nerve to ask her to a school dance that was coming up."

Melissa sensed a sad tale ahead and there was nothing worse than young love scorned. "Did she go to the dance with you?"

He smiled, and she saw a hint of sadness, a whisper of loneliness in the depths of his eyes. "She did. She told me she knew I was rich and if I'd buy her a gold bracelet she'd go with me."

"So you bought her the bracelet?" A tiny pang pieced Melissa's heart, a pain for the boy he'd been who had learned early that his worth was in his wallet.

He nodded. "Bought her the bracelet, took her to the dance and thought it was the beginning of a wonderful love match. Then when I took her home that night she told me that she'd only gone out with me for the bracelet and that I shouldn't bother her anymore." He smiled again and this time it was the smile of the cynic he'd become. "That was my first and only experience with love."

"That's horrible," she exclaimed.

He shrugged. "It was a long time ago. Tell me about the man you were dating before we met that night. Were you in love with him?"

"I believed I was at the time." She thought of Tom, who she'd once thought she would marry. There had been a time when any thought of him brought pain, but all she felt now was relief that she hadn't married a man who had cheated on her, a man who hadn't valued her.

"I loved what I thought we had. I loved the idea of getting married and building a family. I loved the idea of waking up with the same man I went to bed with day after day, year after year. We'd dated for over two years and it had become comfortable. I just assumed we'd take the next step and get married but now I'm glad we didn't. He didn't love me the way I wanted to be loved."

"Mindlessly, desperately," Henry said.

"Exactly," she replied, surprised that he'd remembered she'd said that before.

They fell silent, but it was a comfortable quiet. Melissa sipped her wine and found her gaze going again and again to him.

He was such an attractive man with sharp, bold features and that sexy cleft in his chin. But it wasn't his physical qualities that drew her. She loved the teasing light that so often lit his eyes. She loved the respect and caring he showed to his mother. He was a good man and he would make a wonderful role model for her children.

"I think I'll call it a night," she finally said. "I'm still hoping to be able to get home in the morning." She stood and finished the last of her wine, then headed for the kitchen to place her glass in the sink.

"I think I'll call it a night, too," he said and followed behind her into the kitchen. "Jimmy is coming over tomorrow and we're going to sit down and discuss what's been going on and what we're going to do about it." He placed his glass in the sink next to hers.

"What can you do about it? You don't know who is after you." She looked at him worriedly. "Even if the person is just trying to scare you, there's nothing that says he won't make a mistake and actually manage to shoot you." She was shocked by the fear that rocketed through her, fear for him.

"Yeah, that thought has entered my mind, too," he said dryly. "I'm sure Jimmy and I can put our heads together and come up with a plan to figure out who is responsible and get them behind bars. Don't you worry about it. I'll get it all taken care of."

"I can't help but worry about it," she replied. "You're now a part of my life." Emotion began to well up inside her. "I mean, I don't want my boys to grow up without their father," she said hurriedly.

As they left the kitchen and headed for the stairs, Melissa tried to get her emotions under control. It was true, she didn't want anything to happen to him for the twins' sake. But it was also true that as a woman she'd be devastated if anything happened to him.

He turned off the Christmas tree lights then together they climbed the stairs. As always, the first thing Melissa did when she reached the top of the stairs was go into the boys' bedroom to make sure they were still peacefully sleeping.

Henry followed her in and a soft smile played on his face as he looked first at Joey and then at James. That smile, filled with such love, with such tenderness, created a warmth inside her.

She would never have to worry about her sons being loved. If anything ever happened to her, Henry would make sure they not only had what they needed to survive, but he'd make sure their world had the love he refused to believe in for himself.

"Melissa." He grabbed her hand as they left the room.

She knew immediately what he wanted, what she wanted from him. For months after that night of the blizzard she'd thought about the pleasure she'd found in his arms.

She wanted it again. She wanted him again and she could tell by the heat in his eyes that he wanted the same.

She stepped closer to him and raised her face to him and he took the unspoken invitation by crashing his mouth down on hers.

His mouth was hot hunger against hers and she felt as if she'd been waiting for this since the moment he'd first opened the door to her.

Allowing him to deepen the kiss, she leaned into him, wanting him to have no question in his mind that she wanted him.

His tongue danced with hers as his hands slid down her back and pulled her hips into his. His arousal was evident and fed the flames of desire inside her.

The kiss seemed to last forever before he finally dropped his hands from around her and stepped back. "You look beautiful in that blue sweater, but I remember how beautiful you looked naked. I want you, Melissa. This has nothing to do with anything but you and me."

"I want you, too," she said, her voice a husky whisper.

"You know I'm not making any promises. I need you

to understand that there's no future with me. I'm not the man to give you your happily ever after."

"As far as I'm concerned, tonight you're a handsome cowboy keeping me warm on a wintery night and nothing more," she replied. His eyes flamed as he pulled her into the bedroom and back into his arms.

Chapter 9

This time his kiss left her breathless and aching. When he pulled her sweater over her head she was more than ready for him. There was no embarrassment as she stood before him in her wispy bra. The light from her bathroom spilled into the bedroom and she could see the flames that lit his eyes while he gazed at her.

Every bone in her body weakened and she reached out to unfasten the buttons on his shirt. The heat from his body radiated to her, urging her to unbutton his shirt and sweep it off his broad shoulders.

He was beautiful, with his chiseled chest and flat abdomen. He pulled her back into his arms and as he kissed her he reached around her to unfasten her bra.

He tugged the straps off her shoulders and when it fell away he embraced her again and she delighted in the feel of his bare skin against hers.

"I've wanted this since the moment you arrived," he said, his breath hot against her throat.

"I've wanted it, too," she confessed.

Within minutes they were both naked and beneath the blankets in bed. Even though she'd only made love with him once, his skin felt just the way she remembered, warm and firm as he pulled her against him. The familiar scent of him filled her head and she knew any other man who ever wore that particular brand of cologne would always evoke memories of Henry.

As his kisses made her mindless, his hands cupped her breasts and a low moan escaped her lips. He pulled his mouth from hers and looked down at her. "You are so beautiful," he whispered.

She felt beautiful beneath his gaze. That was part of Henry's gift. He'd made her feel beautiful and desirous that night of the blizzard, and he made her feel that way now.

He lowered his mouth to capture the erect tip of one of her breasts and she tangled her fingers in his rich, dark hair. Sweet sensations sizzled through her.

He teased her nipple, swirling his tongue and using his teeth to lightly nip. Melissa closed her eyes as all concerns about the future melted away beneath the heat of his caresses. She couldn't think about anything but him and the magic of his touch.

She ran her hands down the length of his broad back, loving the play of muscle beneath her fingertips. She felt safe with him, not just physically protected, but emotionally as well. She felt as if she could say anything to him, tell him her deepest, darkest secrets and he'd keep those secrets safe.

The love she'd tried not to feel for him welled up inside her, a love she knew would never be reciprocated. But at the moment that didn't matter. She had this night with him and she knew it had to be enough for her. She wouldn't allow this to happen again but she intended to enjoy every moment of it.

"This is much nicer than a hardwood floor beneath the scratchy blanket from my truck," he said, his voice thick with desire.

"I have very fond memories of that scratchy blanket and the hardwood floor." She could speak no more as his mouth once again claimed hers.

Every inch of her skin was electrified, for each and every place he touched, he kissed, sizzled in response.

His heartbeat was strong and quick against hers, the heart that didn't believe in love, the one that refused to believe that anyone could love him for himself.

She slid her lips down his neck, wanting him to feel loved, to feel as desired as he made her feel. Her mouth moved down his chest and she licked first one of his nipples, then the other.

He gasped, a quick intake of breath that made her even bolder. He rolled over on his back as she moved down the length of his body, kissing and nipping and teasing his fevered skin with her lips.

Tangling his hands in her hair, his entire body tensed as she kissed his inner thigh. He was fully erect and although this was something she'd rarely done for Tom, she wanted the utter intimacy with Henry.

As she took him into her mouth she let out a low groan and every muscle in his body tensed. "Melissa," he moaned as his hands tightened in her hair.

She loved the strained sound of her name on his lips, loved the pleasure she knew she was giving to him. But it didn't take long for him to push her away and roll to his side.

"Now, it's my turn," he said, his eyes gleaming with promise. He ran his hand down her body and rubbed against her. "I want you gasping for air and crying out my name."

As he moved his fingers against the very center of her, a rising tide of pleasure began to build inside her. She arched her hips up to meet his touch, needing release, wanting the wave to consume her.

And then it did, crashing through her as she cried his name over and over again. She shuddered with the force of it and tears filled her eyes. But he wasn't finished yet. He rolled over and grabbed a condom from the night-stand and while she was still weak and gasping, he moved between her legs and entered her.

For a moment neither of them moved. The pleasure

of him filling her up was so intense she feared if she moved she'd lose it again.

He froze, his arms holding him up from her chest. From the light shining in from her bathroom she could see his features. His eyes were closed, his neck muscles corded as if he were under enormous strain.

He opened his eyes and looked down at her, then slowly slid his hips back and thrust forward. That single slow movement broke everything loose between them.

Fast and furious, he stroked into her and she encouraged him by clutching his buttocks and pulling him into her.

Lost. She was lost in him and once again she felt the wild tide rushing in. As it washed over her she felt him tense and moan against her, knowing it had claimed him, too.

He collapsed on her and she wrapped her arms around his back, wishing she could hold him there forever. But all too quickly he got up and padded into the adjoining bathroom.

Melissa turned her head to one side and fought a sudden rush of tears. Of all the foolish, reckless things she'd ever done in her life, this was probably the worst. She'd chosen to make love to a man who apparently wasn't capable of loving her back.

MysteryMom couldn't have known that she was sending Melissa into a new heartbreak. The woman had probably simply wanted to unite a man with his sons, ease the burden of single parenting for Melissa.

She'd accomplished that. Melissa would no longer be alone in the task of raising her sons. She knew in her heart, in her soul, that Henry would always be a support and help in the parenting process.

But MysteryMom couldn't have known that Melissa would fall mindlessly, desperately in love with Henry. She couldn't have known that Melissa would repeat the same mistake that she'd made on that snowy night over a year ago. At least he'd used a condom and there wouldn't be another accidental pregnancy.

As he came out of the bathroom she assumed he'd leave to go to his bedroom, but instead he surprised her by sliding back beneath the sheets and taking her in his arms. He kissed her on the temple, a sweet, soft kiss that touched her more than anything that had occurred between them.

"Definitely better in a bed," he said. He lay on his back and pulled her into his side. His hand stroked her hair as she placed her head on his chest. "I really hate to see you take off tomorrow."

"It's time, Henry. It's been a wonderful holiday but now it's over and I have to get back to my real life." It was more important than ever that she leave here as soon as possible. Her heart had gotten involved in a way that already would ache when she left. More time here would only make the ache sharper when she did go home.

She raised her head to look at him. "You know I'll do whatever I can to make it easy on you to see the boys."

"I know that." He raised his hand and trailed a finger

down the side of her cheek, across her lower lip. "I can't think of a better woman to be the mother of my boys."

The tears that had hovered just under the surface sprang to her eyes at his words. "You're just saying that now because you have me naked in bed with you," she replied with a choked little laugh.

"You know that's not true," he chided. "You have the values I want the boys to have. I know you'll teach them to have integrity, to have strong but gentle hearts."

She ran her hand across his chest and placed it on his heart. Her last thought before she fell asleep was that the one thing she would teach her boys was to believe in the power and wonder of love, something apparently nobody had ever taught Henry.

Henry stood at the window in his study and watched the snow swirling in the air. It had snowed about two inches overnight, effectively postponing Melissa's plans to leave first thing that morning.

He was now waiting for Jimmy to arrive. Jimmy had called earlier to tell Henry that the snow wouldn't keep him from his appointment.

Staring at the carriage house in the distance, Henry thought of the night before. Making love to Melissa had been amazing and he'd been in no hurry to leave her bed.

Henry couldn't remember the last time he'd slept with a woman in his arms. He'd never stayed the night with Hilary, had always preferred the comfort of being alone in his own bed. But sleeping with Melissa had been not just comfortable, but comforting in a way he'd never imagined. It had been nice to feel the warmth of her next to him as he'd drifted off to sleep. And it had been equally as nice to wake up with her curled in his arms.

Surely these crazy feelings he was developing for her were nothing more than gratitude. After all, she'd given him the greatest gift a man could get—children.

He wasn't going to mention the carriage house solution to her again. He recognized that over the past two days he'd become a bore and bordered on becoming a bully in trying to get her to do what he wanted.

Whatever she decided, they'd make it work because it had to work. Even though they weren't married, he knew they'd do whatever was in the best interest of the twins.

At the moment Melissa and his mother and the twins were all in the kitchen. It was Etta's day off and they were in the process of making dinner.

As he'd walked to his study he'd heard the sound of laughter and merriment coming from the kitchen. The house would feel empty once Melissa and the boys were gone.

Actually, the house had felt empty for a long time. And if he thought about it long enough he'd admit that his life had been fairly empty for a very long time. He frowned, irritated with the direction his thoughts were taking. Maybe it was a good thing Melissa was leaving soon. She was messing with his mind in a way that was distinctly uncomfortable.

He turned away from the window as a knock fell on

his door. The door opened and Jimmy poked his head in. "Your mom told me to come on in," he said.

Henry motioned him inside. "How are the roads?" he asked as he gestured his friend into the chair in front of the desk.

"A little nasty but not too bad. The road crews are out working so if we don't get any more accumulation we should have everything under control." He eased into the chair. "You got any of that good scotch hidden away in here?"

Henry walked to the minibar in the corner and poured himself and Jimmy a drink, then handed Jimmy his and sat at the desk with his own.

Jimmy took a deep swallow and sighed. "I don't know if Willie told you or not, but he found the bullet that shot out your tire still in the rubber that was left on the truck. It was a .22 caliber. I know it wasn't Hank. At the time your truck was fired on, Hank was down at Lazy Ed's, completely sauced."

Lazy Ed's was a popular tavern for the ranch hands in the area. "I'm not surprised. His drinking is what caused him to get fired in the first place," Henry said.

"Before we get into all this, I want to know about those twin boys that your mother introduced me to in the kitchen. They sure do have the Randolf chin. You been holding out on me about your love life?"

Henry smiled and knew in an instant he wasn't about to tell Jimmy the truth about how the twins were conceived. Although Henry certainly wasn't a prude, he didn't want to give anyone in town a reason to think less of Melissa.

"Melissa is a friend from Amarillo. She's a terrific woman and we've been close for some time. When she got pregnant we agreed that we'd share the parenting of the boys and remain friends."

"I never even knew you wanted kids," Jimmy said.

Henry smiled. "I didn't know I wanted them until they were here. I got to tell you, Jimmy. They change your life. They make you want to be a better man. That's why it's so important we get this mess cleaned up, these attacks that are happening on me. I can't have them around if it's not safe."

Henry leaned back in his chair. "You know who is at the top of my suspect list."

Jimmy nodded. "Tom Burke. You scare him, Henry."

"He should be scared," Henry said with a scowl. "You and I both know he's a criminal."

Jimmy nodded. "I've been in contact with the FBI and I'm hoping they're going to look into his actions as city manager. The problem is we both know he's a likely suspect. What we don't have is any proof."

"Did you question him about his whereabouts at the time my tire was shot out?"

Jimmy nodded. "According to his wife, he was at home with her."

Once again Henry frowned. "You know damn good and well she'd lie for him."

Jimmy nodded. "I've put a couple of my men on

Tom. Full-time surveillance as long as I have the manpower. If he tries anything we'll be on top of him. It's the best I can do, Henry."

Henry nodded. He knew Jimmy was as frustrated as he was by what had been happening. He took a drink of his scotch.

"If this had all started the night that Melissa showed up here with those babies, I would ask you if you thought Hilary might be playing a woman scorned," Jimmy said.

Henry laughed at the very idea of Hilary hiding out in the woods with a gun. "No way. I'll grant you she wasn't too happy to discover I had two babies, but Hilary knew the score where I was concerned. Besides, she'd never risk breaking a nail to do anything like this."

"And the first attack happened to you before Melissa arrived on the scene," Jimmy said.

Henry nodded. "I'm telling you it's Tom Burke or it's somebody he's hired. He's the only person who has a hell of a lot to lose if I become mayor."

Jimmy tilted his glass up for another drink of the scotch. "I just wanted to come out here and tell you that I'm doing the best I can."

"What about a ballistics test on the bullet Willie dug out of my tire?" Henry asked.

"Unfortunately the bullet hit your rim and was pretty mangled. Besides, in order to do a ballistics test you have to have a weapon to compare it to and Tom Burke insists he doesn't have a rifle."

Henry snorted in disbelief. "I don't know a man in this entire county who doesn't own a rifle. This is Texas, for God's sake."

"You're preaching to the choir, Henry."

For the next thirty minutes the men spoke about other potential suspects. There were only two that Henry could think of, both council members and friends of Tom Burke.

"You definitely have the support of the people," Jimmy said. "People like you, they admire your integrity and they trust you. If you can stay alive until February there is no doubt in my mind that you'll be voted in as mayor."

"That's nice to hear," Henry replied.

Jimmy glanced toward the window. "I've got to head back into town." He stood.

"I appreciate you coming out on such a crummy day." Henry stood as well.

"I swear I'm going to get to the bottom of this, Henry," Jimmy said as they left the study.

"I just hope you do before this mysterious shooter gets lucky," Henry said dryly.

The two men walked to the front door, where they said their goodbyes. The snow had begun to fall again and as Henry closed the door he realized that he was more worried now about whoever was trying to hurt him than he'd been before Melissa had arrived in the house.

Before, he'd just been irritated by the whole thing. But now all he could think about was if anything happened to him the boys wouldn't have their father. He had every reason in the world to want to stay alive…for them and for Melissa.

The laughter coming from the kitchen pulled him away from the front door and to the source of the sound. Once there he found his mother and Melissa finishing up dinner preparations.

As he walked into the room, the twins flashed him smiles that as always filled him with warmth. "Something smells wonderful," he said.

"Melissa can cook," Mary exclaimed.

"It's just spaghetti with meat sauce," Melissa replied as she took a pot of boiling pasta off the stove top.

Henry took a seat at the table and watched as she dumped the spaghetti noodles into an awaiting colander. "You don't understand. Mom would think you were amazing if you could just boil an egg. She's the worst cook in the entire state of Texas."

Melissa shot a quick glance to Mary. "Don't worry," Mary said with a laugh. "He's quite right. It's one of the reasons Big Henry hired Etta. He knew if we tried to live on my cooking we'd all starve. Henry, why don't you set the table and I'll get the salad."

As always, dinner was a pleasant time. They chatted about favorite foods and Mary regaled Melissa with some of her war stories at the stove. The boys kept up their end of the conversation by babbling and cooing.

At one point James blew a raspberry. He looked startled and as they all laughed, he grinned and blew another one.

Henry smiled at Melissa. "You might have gotten his very first smile, but at least I didn't miss out on his very first raspberry."

After they'd finished eating Mary took the boys into the living room while Henry and Melissa cleaned up. "Dinner was terrific," he said as he stacked the dishes she rinsed into the dishwasher. "Do you like to cook?"

She nodded. "I do, but most of the time it seems like a lot of trouble to cook for one. When my mother was alive I did a lot of cooking, but not so much since she passed."

"You miss her."

She smiled with a touch of sadness. "Every day. Unfortunately diabetes is a ruthless disease and I think she was tired of fighting. It's some comfort to know she's not in pain anymore."

"I miss my father, too. He and I weren't just father and son, we were friends." Henry smiled at thoughts of his dad. "He was bigger than life, one of those colorful characters that people didn't forget after meeting him."

Melissa handed him the last plate. "And he taught you everything you need to know about being a wonderful father."

Henry smiled. "Yeah, I hadn't thought about it before, but he was a wonderful role model." He took the towel she offered him and dried his hands.

"It worried me that I was all alone," she said, her expression somber. "I worried about what would happen to the boys if I got hit by a car or had a sudden heart attack. Now I don't have to worry anymore. I know if anything happens to me you'll love them and take care of them."

"Nothing is going to happen to you," he assured her. "You and I are going to parent those boys until they're hulking adults and we're old and gray."

She smiled. "I like that plan, and speaking of the boys, I think it's probably time for a diaper change."

The rest of the evening passed and by nine o'clock it was time to put the boys down for the night. Mary said her good-night and retired to her wing of the house while Melissa carried Joey and Henry carried James up the stairs to their room.

Once the boys were settled into their beds, Melissa motioned Henry into her room. "Do you think I'm going to be able to head home tomorrow?" she asked.

Henry walked over to her window and peered outside. A light snow was still falling. He turned to look at her. "Why don't you make a decision in the morning? It's snowing now but maybe it will stop before too long. I can call Jimmy in the morning and ask him about the condition of the roads."

What he really wanted to do was have a repeat of the night before. But something in the way she stood with her arms crossed in front of her chest made him think she wouldn't be open to the idea.

"You want to go back down and have a glass of wine or something?" he asked.

She shook her head. "No, I think I'll just call it a night

now. I really am hoping that we'll be able to travel in the morning. Besides, it's been a long day and I'm exhausted."

He realized she was already distancing herself, preparing for the goodbye. He was surprised at the edge of sadness that took hold of him. It wasn't like it was going to be goodbye forever, he told himself. Most likely one way or another he'd be seeing her every weekend. If she didn't want to drive here, then he'd drive to Amarillo. But somehow he knew that once she left here things would never be the same between them again.

"Then I guess I'll just say good night," he said. He couldn't help himself. He stepped closer to her with the intention to deliver a kiss to her forehead, but instead found his mouth claiming hers.

The minute their lips connected the window where Henry had stood moments before shattered. As Henry saw the device that lay on the floor in the bedroom fear screamed inside him.

He shoved Melissa toward the door and they fell into the hallway as the bomb went off.

Chapter 10

One moment Henry had been kissing her and the next Melissa found herself on the hallway floor with Henry on top of her. The back of her head had connected hard with the floor in the fall and she was dazed and confused.

The loud explosion still rang in Melissa's ears, making her momentarily deaf. As Henry got off her, her hearing began to return. Above the din of the house alarm ringing she could hear the cries of her babies and her heart slammed into her chest with enough force to steal what little breath she had left.

"Check on the boys," Henry yelled as he pulled her up off the floor. He raced back into the bedroom and tore down the curtains that had caught on fire. As he stamped out the flames, she ran across the hall to the boys' room. They were safe, but scared by the noise.

She took them into her arms, and her heart beat so fast it felt as if it were trying to burst out of her chest. She stood in the center of the room, afraid to move, unsure what might happen next. She tried to calm the boys but with the alarm ringing discordantly it was impossible. Tears raced down Melissa's cheeks as she tried to still her own fear.

Somebody had thrown a bomb of some kind into the window of the bedroom where she'd slept, at the window where Henry had been standing only moments earlier. Her head couldn't wrap around it.

The blast could have killed him. It could have killed her. Had Henry not reacted as quickly as he had, they both could have been seriously hurt or worse.

She hugged the boys even closer to her chest and breathed a sigh of relief as the alarm suddenly stopped ringing. Now what? Had the danger passed? Was there more to come? Too afraid to move, she remained in the center of the room.

A moment later both Henry and Mary rushed into the room.

"You okay?" Henry asked her, his features taut with tension.

"We're fine," she said and felt a new press of tears as Mary put an arm around her shoulder.

"Jimmy is on his way," Henry said as he took Joey from her arms. "Let's go downstairs to wait for him."

By the time they got down the stairs several of Henry's ranch hands were at the front door. Henry opened the door to allow them inside and they all gathered in the living room.

"We heard the explosion," Charlie said, his features grim. "Then we saw the fire at the window. I'm just glad to see you're all okay."

"You didn't see anyone?" Henry asked as he shifted Joey from one arm to the other.

Both Charlie and Randy shook their heads. "Didn't hear a car, didn't see a soul," Charlie said. "Dammit, it's like it's a phantom."

"It wasn't a phantom that threw a bomb through the window," Henry said, his anger rife in his voice. He handed Joey to his mother. "I want to go out and take a look around. With the snow there should be some footprints that can be tracked."

Charlie frowned. "Unfortunately, Randy and I might have messed up any prints," he admitted. "When we heard the blast we both ran to that side of the house. I didn't even think about footprints."

"There still might be some prints that don't belong to the two of you," Henry said.

"Please, Henry, wait for Jimmy before you go out," Melissa said. She had no idea what other danger might await him if he ventured outside and she couldn't stand the thought of anything happening to him.

"Yes, Henry," Mary spoke up, her voice filled with

a mother's worry. "Please wait for Jimmy. I don't want you out there."

Melissa could tell by Henry's expression that he was chomping at the bit, needing to do something, anything that might find the guilty party.

"If you want, Randy and I can go back out and take another look around," Charlie offered.

"Trust me, if there's anyone around I'd be happy to tie him up and beat his ass until Jimmy shows up," Randy exclaimed.

Henry clapped him on the back. "I appreciate the sentiment, Randy, but the last thing I want is for anyone to get hurt. Why don't we all sit tight until Jimmy gets here?"

Charlie and Randy sat on the two chairs while Melissa and Mary sat on the sofa with the twins. Henry paced the room, looking like he wanted nothing more than to punch something or someone.

There was no question that somehow, someway, Melissa had to leave here as soon as possible. She couldn't place her children at risk. The idea that the pipe bomb could have easily been thrown through the window of the bedroom where the twins slept filled her with a kind of terror she'd never felt before.

"Randy, what I'd like you to do is see if you can find a piece of plywood in the shed to put over the broken window after Jimmy takes a look around." Henry turned to look at Melissa and his eyes were dark as midnight. "Melissa, I want you to pack a bag for you and the boys."

She looked at him in surprise. "But where are we

going?" She knew the roads were snow-packed and her tires weren't in the best shape. There was no way she'd take off at this time of night for home.

"I'm going to have Charlie check you in to a motel until the roads are safe enough for you to travel home." Henry looked at his mother. "You might want to pack a bag, too."

"Nonsense," Mary scoffed. "I agree with you that Melissa should take the twins and go but nobody is chasing me out of my home."

Henry nodded, as if unsurprised by his mother's decision to stay put. He returned his attention to Melissa. "The latest weather report I heard said that the snow is going to stick around for at least another twenty-four to forty-eight hours, so pack enough things to last you and the boys for a couple of days."

"But what about you?" Melissa asked. She wanted him to come with them, to leave this place of danger and hide out with her someplace where she knew he'd be safe.

"I'll be fine as long as I know you and the twins are safe." He took James from her arms. "Come on, I'll go up and help you get your things together."

"I'm going to head out to the shed," Randy said. "It's been long enough now I imagine whoever threw that bomb is long gone."

"And I'll wait here with Mrs. Randolf," Charlie added.

Henry said nothing as they climbed the stairs back to the room where the blast had occurred. The scent of smoke and gasoline lingered in the air.

"It must have been loaded with fuel," he said as he

surveyed the damage. "At least it wasn't filled with any kind of shrapnel."

Melissa shuddered at the thought. She pulled her suitcase from the closet and quickly packed what little she'd brought with her. They then moved into the boys' room, where she packed their clothes and diapers.

"I'll have Charlie get you settled in at one of the motels and I'll call you first thing in the morning," he said. She turned to face him and saw the worry in his eyes, a worry coupled with rage.

He stepped up to her and placed his palm against her cheek. She turned her face into the warmth of his hand. "He could have hurt you tonight. He could have hurt you and the boys."

"But that didn't happen," she said softly.

"Not this time, but I can't take another chance. I thought you were safe here, but I now realize I can't guarantee your safety. You'll be safe in a motel until the roads are clean enough for you to go home."

"Henry?" Jimmy's voice drifted up the stairs.

Henry dropped his hand from her face and stepped back from her. "Come on up, Jimmy."

Melissa and Henry met the lawman in the hallway. "You can have a look around. I'm sending Melissa with Charlie to a motel for the rest of the night. I'll be back up here as soon as I get those arrangements made."

Henry didn't say a word as they went back downstairs. Once there, as Melissa and Mary began to put the coats on the boys, he disappeared into his study.

Minutes later he came out. "I've got you set up in a room at Ed's Motel. It's clean and comfortable and the owner is a friend of mine. The room is registered in the name of Hank James. Nobody will know you're there and the key will be waiting for you in the office."

A muscle knotted in his jaw. "Charlie will get you there safe and sound and I'll call you in the morning." He shoved a wad of cash into her hand. "There's a diner right next door to the motel. They'll deliver whatever you need to your motel-room door."

It was crazy, but as Melissa pulled on her coat and Charlie grabbed her bags, she had a sudden terrible fear for Henry.

"Please, stay safe," she said as she held the twins in her arms.

He kissed Joey and James on the forehead and then gently shoved a strand of her hair behind her ear. "Get out of here and let me do what I need to do."

It took only minutes for her and the boys to be loaded into Charlie's four-wheel-drive vehicle. While they pulled away from the house Melissa looked back to see Henry silhouetted in the front door.

Once again she was struck with the strong, inexplicable fear—the fear that she was never going to see him again.

"Henry, where are you going?" Jimmy asked as Henry pulled on his winter coat. They had just spent the last hour picking through the rubble in the bedroom.

Jimmy had collected the pieces of the device to use as evidence and now Randy was hanging the plywood over the broken window.

Charlie had returned to the ranch after dropping Melissa and the children at Ed's Motel. At least Henry had the comfort of knowing she and the babies would be safe there until she could leave town.

With each moment that had ticked by a rage had grown in Henry, a seething sick rage that begged to be released. And he knew exactly where to vent it.

"I'm going to Burke's house." Henry buttoned his coat but didn't reach for his gun in the drawer. He knew if he had it on him he might use it and as much as he wanted to hurt the man he believed was responsible for the pipe bomb, he didn't want to kill him. He was a father now, a man who had too much too lose by letting his rage get the best of him.

"Dammit, Henry, you can't go off half-cocked," Jimmy exclaimed in frustration.

"Trust me, I'm not half-cocked, I'm fully loaded," Henry replied dryly.

"Just stay put," Jimmy said. "I'll go talk to Burke."

"Then I'm coming with you." Henry didn't give Jimmy another opportunity to talk him out of it, but instead slammed out the door and walked into the snowy night.

Minutes later he and Jimmy were in Jimmy's patrol car navigating the slick roads as they headed into town. All Henry could think about was how devastating the results might have been had that bomb been thrown into the boys' room. The thought of such a tragedy stoked the flames of his rage even hotter.

"He could have killed my kids, Jimmy. He could have killed Melissa," Henry said, breaking the silence in the car.

"I know," Jimmy said. He grunted as the back of the car threatened to fishtail out. He steered into the slide and straightened the car. "We'll check out Tom's alibi for the time that the bomb was thrown through the window."

"It's possible he didn't personally throw it, but instead hired somebody." Henry frowned. "I've got to put an end to this." He stared out into the dark night. "Maybe I should withdraw from the election."

Jimmy shot him a stunned look. "You'd do that?"

"If I just had myself to worry about then I'd never quit. But it's not just me anymore, Jimmy. I've got kids and Melissa and they are going to need me."

"So they win and the corruption in Dalhart continues." Jimmy released an audible sigh. "Just give me a few more days before you make a decision. You're running on pure emotion right now. Give yourself time to calm down and let me sort this out."

Henry didn't reply. He knew Jimmy was right. He was definitely running on emotion, but as he thought of Melissa and Joey and James, he couldn't help but be filled with emotion.

He'd wanted to be a hero to the town, to clean up the mess that had been allowed to go on for far too long.

But he now wondered if the stakes were too high. He'd rather be a father than a hero.

He sat up straighter in the seat as they approached town. The only other vehicles they'd passed were snow trucks laying down salt and pushing snow.

Tom Burke lived well above his means and salary in a five-bedroom luxury home on a three-acre lot. The first thing Henry noticed was that Tom's car was parked in the driveway. Not only was the car relatively clean of snow, but tire tracks showed that it had recently been driven.

The rage that had slowly begun to wane during the drive now roared back to life inside Henry. He was out of the car before it had come to a complete halt.

"Henry, dammit, wait for me," Jimmy cried as he parked the car and got out.

Henry didn't wait. He headed for the front door with a single-mindedness and once he got there he banged on the door with his fist.

By the time the door was opened by Tom, Jimmy had reached the porch. Henry didn't say a word, but rather grabbed the short man by the front of his pristine white shirt and dragged him out the door.

"Hey, get your hands off me," Tom yelled and jerked out of Henry's grasp. "What the hell is wrong with you, man?"

"Have you been out to my place tonight, Tom? I see your car has been driven. Did you come to pay me a little visit?" Henry glared at him and became aware of Deputy Gordon Hunter joining them on the porch.

"I don't know what you're talking about," Tom exclaimed, his beefy face red. "I haven't been anywhere near your place tonight."

"Then you hired somebody to throw that pipe bomb through my window." Henry took a menacing step toward him. "I had babies in the house, you bastard."

Tom looked from Henry to Jimmy. "A pipe bomb? I don't know a damn thing about a pipe bomb."

"Then where did you go tonight?" Henry demanded. "Your car has been driven recently. Where did you go?"

"To the damned grocery store," Tom exclaimed in frustration. "We're supposed to get more snow. I needed to get a gallon of milk. Is that a crime now?"

"It's true," Gordon said. "I've been watching him, tailing him all evening. The only place he went is to the grocery store."

Henry stared at Gordon, then back at Tom. "I'm warning you right now, Tom. If anything happens to anyone I care about, I'll be back here to see you and I'll beat your ass to a pulp."

Tom looked at Jimmy in outrage. "Did you hear that? He threatened me with bodily harm."

Jimmy shook his head. "Nah, he didn't threaten you. He promised you." Jimmy clapped his hand on Henry's back. "Come on, Henry, nothing more can be done here for now."

Henry shot Tom another killer glare, then stalked back to Jimmy's car and got into the passenger seat. As

Jimmy and Gordon spoke to Tom for another few minutes, Henry steamed.

How were they ever going to get to the bottom of this? Whoever was responsible was smart enough to leave no clues behind, to do the kind of sneak attacks that made it impossible to investigate.

One thing was clear. He couldn't allow Melissa and the boys back into his home until the situation was resolved and that angered him more than anything.

It was a tension-filled ride back home. Jimmy talked the whole way, detailing his plan to investigate what had happened.

"We might be able to find fingerprints on the pieces of the bomb that survived the blast. There might be specific traceable material that was used. Don't you worry, Henry. I'm going to get to the bottom of this."

As he babbled on, Henry stared out the window, his mind drifting to Melissa and the boys. What were they doing at this moment? He glanced at his watch and realized his sons would be sound asleep and tonight he wouldn't be able to stand in the doorway and smell their scent, watch their little faces as they dreamed. Tonight he and Melissa wouldn't be able to sit together in the living room, enjoying quiet conversation after his mother had gone to bed.

The fact that some nut had taken these particular pleasures away from him reignited the fire of his anger. But by the time they finally reached the house the anger had burned itself out and he was simply exhausted.

Randy and Charlie sat with his mother in the living room and he quickly told them what had happened with Tom, then Charlie and Randy left.

"Are you all right?" his mother asked as he walked to the bar and poured himself a healthy dose of scotch.

"No. I'm angry and frustrated and I'm wondering if I shouldn't just pull out of the election." He sat on the sofa next to her.

"Is that what you want to do?"

"I don't want anything to happen to Melissa and the boys."

Mary smiled at him. "That didn't answer my question. Besides, as soon as the roads clear Melissa and the boys will return to Amarillo. You still have to live here with any decision you make."

Henry released a sigh and dropped his head back against the cushion. "I've never really been scared in my life, but the thought of how close danger came to Melissa and the boys put a fear in my heart I never want to feel again."

"Parenthood brings with it a multitude of fears." Mary patted his hand. "The first time those boys get on a bicycle your heart is going to race with fear. The day you put them on a bus to go to school you're going to be filled with a terror as you think of all the things that can go wrong. But you'll also know a joy greater than anything you've ever experienced with them."

Henry nodded.

"And then there's Melissa," Mary said softly. "You light up in her presence, Henry."

"She's the mother of my children," he replied.

"I think she could be more than that to you if you'd just open up that heart of yours," Mary said.

"I don't want her to be any more than that," he replied with forced lightness.

Mary sighed. "Your father was a wonderful man, Henry, but he was obsessed about some woman stealing your money. I worry that instead of making you careful, which was his intention, he made you incapable of allowing anyone close to you."

He was in no mood for one of his mother's attempts to get him to change his mind about love and marriage. He tipped his glass up and drained his drink, welcoming the hot burn down his throat. "Mom, it's been a long day and I'm exhausted. I have a lot of things to think about and I don't want to have a conversation about my decision to stay single."

"You're right. I'm sorry." She got up from the sofa. "I'm going to bed. I'll see you in the morning and hopefully by then Jimmy will have this all figured out and we can get back to a normal life."

"Good night, Mom." He watched her disappear up the stairs, then once again leaned his head back and released a long sigh.

He hoped Jimmy had some answers in the morning, but he didn't expect him to have any. He looked over at the phone. What he'd like to do is call Melissa, just hear her voice before he called it a night. But it was late and he didn't want to wake the boys. Besides, he'd told her he'd call her first thing in the morning.

He got up from the sofa and walked to the window. It was snowing again. Yesterday he'd hoped for snow so that he could keep Melissa and the boys here longer. Now he prayed for it to end so she could take the boys back to Amarillo where they would be safe from the madness that had become his life.

Chapter 11

It was the longest night of Melissa's life. The motel room was typical of motel rooms all around the country, equipped with a king-size bed, a television in a cabinet and a desk. It was spotlessly clean and once she'd placed the desk chair and a barricade of pillows along one side of the bed, the boys fell asleep almost immediately.

Unfortunately sleep remained elusive for her. She took a fast shower and changed into her nightgown, then got into bed and tried not to relive the events of the night.

What was happening at the house? Were Henry and Mary all right? If anything happened who would come to tell Melissa that something had gone wrong? Surely somebody would keep her informed.

She tossed and turned with worry and fear and it was during those long hours of sleeplessness that she realized the depth of her love for Henry James Randolf III. And in that realization she knew she would never be able to give him what he wanted.

The idea of making her home in the carriage house, so close, yet not a part of his life, was physically painful to consider. She could easily imagine the kind of routine they'd fall into over time.

The twins would spend a lot of their time in the big house with Henry and Mary and occasionally the desire Henry and Melissa felt for each other would rear up and explode and they'd make love. There would be no commitment, no love, just an arrangement. She couldn't do it. She couldn't sacrifice her own dreams of a marriage and love forever just so that Henry could get what he wanted—full-time access to the boys and an occasional release of sexual tension with her.

As soon as possible she was heading home and she and Henry would work out a viable visitation plan, one that didn't involve her living in his backyard.

She finally fell asleep around dawn and awakened around eight with a sliver of sunshine drifting in around the edges of the curtains. The boys were still asleep. The disruption from the night before had apparently exhausted them.

She got out of bed and pulled on the luxurious burgundy robe Henry had bought her and moved to the window to peer outside. Although it had snowed another inch or so overnight, the sun was a welcome sight. Surely by late evening or first thing in the morning the roads would be cleared enough that she and the babies could go home.

She needed the reality of her little apartment, away from Henry, where she could think clearly. Being with Henry definitely muddied her mind.

The ring of the telephone on the desk pulled her from the window. She grabbed up the receiver and said a soft hello.

"You okay?" Henry's deep voice filled her ear.

"I am now that I know you're okay," she replied. "I couldn't sleep last night. I've been worried about you."

"I almost called you last night to tell you that everything was fine, but I was afraid I'd wake the boys. I've got a glass company coming out first thing this morning to replace the broken window in the bedroom. Jimmy and his men went over it with a fine-tooth comb looking for anything that might be evidentiary. How are the boys?"

She glanced over to the bed. "Still sleeping. What happened after I left last night?" She listened as he told her about going to Tom Burke's home and confronting the man he thought responsible.

"You didn't really expect him to confess, did you?" she asked when he was finished.

"No, but it would have been nice if we could have settled all this last night. I'm hoping Jimmy will be able to get something from the pieces of the device he collected last night, something that will be enough evidence for an arrest."

"You know I can't come back to the house," she said, her heart heavy as the words left her mouth.

"I don't want you and the boys back here," he replied. "Not until this is all resolved. Last night was too close for comfort and I'd never forgive myself if anything happened to you or Joey or James."

Melissa squeezed the receiver closer to her ear as she heard the passion in his voice. He cared about her. She knew he did, but it wasn't enough for him to invite her fully into his life.

"You have everything you need there? The roads are still pretty bad but you should be able to get home sometime tomorrow."

"That's what I thought when I looked outside the window a minute ago, and yes, I have everything I need—we need."

"I'll have Charlie or one of the other men deliver your car later today or first thing in the morning. I don't want to be seen there with you." He paused a moment. "So I won't be able to tell you or the boys a personal goodbye."

She could hear the regret, a true longing in his voice, but she was almost glad that there wouldn't be a personal goodbye. There were going to be enough goodbyes in their future and she had a feeling she'd find each and every one of them difficult. "You'll let me know if anything changes?"

"Of course," he replied. "I'll call you later this evening in any case. And, Melissa, I'm so sorry about all this."

"You don't have to apologize. Just take care of yourself, Henry. My boys need their daddy."

"And I need them," he replied softly, then with a murmured goodbye he hung up. By that time the boys were awakening and she changed diapers and fixed them each a bottle of formula.

While they ate their breakfast she made a pot of coffee in the coffeemaker provided, then studied the menu she found on the desk from the diner next door.

She was starving and she knew part of it was probably stress-related. She picked up the phone and called in an order for an omelet and toast. While she waited for the food to be delivered she got dressed for the day.

The boys had just finished their bottles when her food was delivered. She sat at the desk to eat and kept one eye on the twins, who entertained themselves by playing with their fingers and toes and gurgling to each other as if sharing a secret language.

The omelet was excellent and after she'd cleaned up the mess she stretched out on the bed and played with her sons.

Maybe it had just been the spirit of Christmas that had her feeling so strongly about Henry. The days she had spent in his home had been like a fantasy of everything she'd ever wanted in her life. She didn't care about the lavish gifts or the fancy mansion; she didn't care about personal cooks and sterling silverware. She didn't need any of that.

It had been the warmth of family that had seduced her, the caring both Mary and Henry had offered to her and her children. It had been the shared laughter and the comfortable small talk.

Henry was going to make a tremendous father, but he'd warned her all along that he wasn't interested in becoming a husband. Still, somehow he'd made her want to be his wife.

Instead of thinking of what would never be, she tried to focus on what she intended to do when she got home. She was more determined than ever to jump back into her decorating business. She'd contact old clients, solicit for new ones and hopefully the business would grow.

Somehow she and Henry would work out a solution to the visitation issue, one that would allow each of them the independence to continue their own lives. Eventually perhaps she would find a man who would love her like she wanted to be loved, a man who would bind his life with hers. Although at the moment the idea of any man other than Henry filled her with repugnance.

What she'd once felt for Tom was a pale imitation of her feelings for Henry. She realized now that she hadn't loved Tom. She'd never loved like she loved Henry.

The day passed achingly slow. When the boys fell asleep for their naps, she turned on the television and watched two soap operas that she'd never seen before.

Around four o'clock she placed another order at the diner, deciding that an early meal and early bedtime would be the best thing.

The sun had continued to shine throughout the day and she'd heard the rumble of street plows working, letting her know that she should be able to leave first thing in the morning.

By five-thirty she'd eaten her dinner, fed the boys and the sun had gone down. She was considering changing back into her nightgown when a knock fell on her door.

With the chain on the door she cracked it open a mere inch to see who was on the other side. "Charlie," she said and quickly unfastened the chain to open the door. "Henry said you might come by to bring my car."

"Actually, Henry sent me here to take you and the boys back to the house," Charlie replied as he stepped inside the room.

"What?" She looked at him in surprise. "Has something happened?"

Charlie nodded. "Tom Burke has been arrested and the danger is over. Henry wants you all back at the ranch."

"When did all this happen?" she asked, a wave of happiness sweeping through her.

"Just a little while ago. I don't have any real details. Henry just told me to come here and collect you and the boys and bring you home."

Melissa looked around the room. "It's going to take a few minutes for me to pack everything up again."

Charlie smiled. "Take your time. I just know Henry doesn't want you here another night since it's safe now for you to be back at the house."

Melissa was thrilled by the news that Tom had been arrested and Henry was no longer in danger. Charlie entertained the twins with silly faces while Melissa scurried around and quickly packed her things.

She was going to have to say goodbye in person. The thought broke her heart just a little bit. It would have been easier to take off in the morning without any long goodbyes to Henry. But she knew Henry probably wanted to spend time with the twins one last time before she left for home the next day.

Tonight she would have to tell him about her decision not to move into the carriage house. It would be difficult but she was firm in her decision and he was just going to have to accept it.

Finally she had her things ready to go. While Charlie carried her suitcase back to his SUV, she got the boys into their coats. "You're going to see Daddy again," she said, buttoning Joey's coat.

"I'll carry this little guy," Charlie said as he came back into the room and picked up James. "I've still got the car seats so everyone will ride safely."

Within minutes they were all packed in the car and Charlie started the engine. "Do I need to check out or anything?" she asked.

"Nah, Henry will take care of it." He put the vehicle in Reverse and backed out of the parking space.

"So you don't know what kind of charges have been pressed again Tom?" she asked.

"No, but I'm assuming it's attempted murder or something serious like that," Charlie replied.

"I'm so happy that it's finally been resolved, that Henry is safe and can get on with his life." She stared out the window and frowned. "Shouldn't we be going the opposite direction?"

"No, I'm going exactly where I need to go." Charlie turned and smiled at her, but in the depths of his eyes she saw something cold, something calculating and the first whisper of fear edged through her.

Her throat went dry. "Do you have an errand to run before you take us home?"

"Yeah, an errand that's going to change my life." He reached into his coat pocket and pulled out a gun. "And I suggest you sit back and enjoy the ride."

Melissa stared at him with a rising sense of horror. Charlie? Why was Charlie holding a gun on her and where was he taking her?

Fear screamed inside her head, a fear for herself, but more important, a fear for the two babies who were in the backseat.

It had been a busy day but no matter what Henry did his thoughts were on Melissa and the boys. It ached in him that he wouldn't be able to give the boys a final kiss on their sweet cheeks before sending them back home, that he wouldn't be able to fill his lungs with the sweet baby scent of them.

He would have liked the opportunity to tell Melissa goodbye in person, too. One last look at that shine in her eyes, one more of her lovely smiles to end the holidays would have been nice.

But he reminded himself that this wasn't a permanent goodbye. Whether they liked it or not they were in each other's lives for at least the next eighteen years.

Etta hadn't made it in because of the snow so at dinnertime he and his mother had a quiet meal of ham and cheese sandwiches. In fact, throughout the day the house had been far too quiet.

He hadn't realized how much Melissa and the boys had filled it up and brightened every dark corner. He told himself this was just temporary, that eventually they'd be back and the house would come alive once again.

It was almost six o'clock when he sat down in his study and picked up the phone to call her. The phone rang at the motel room once…twice…three times. Henry frowned as it rang a fourth and fifth time.

He finally hung up but stared at the phone with confusion. Surely she wouldn't have taken the boys out anywhere. She didn't have a car and it was frigid outside. *Maybe she's in the shower,* he thought.

Picking up a pen, he tapped the end of it on his desk as a vision of Melissa in the shower filled his head. He could easily imagine her slender body beneath a steaming spray of water, visualize the slide of the soap across her full breasts.

He threw the pen down, irritated with these kinds of thoughts. He'd believed that if he made love to her one more time she'd be out of his system. He thought that the crazy physical attraction he felt for her would wane, but instead of diminishing, it seemed to have grown stronger.

He picked up the phone and tried her number again. It rang and rang and still there was no answer. How long did a woman spend in the shower?

He got up from the desk and paced the room, a thrum of anxiety inside his chest. Moving to the window, he stared out in the direction of the carriage house. He still hoped to talk her into moving in there. It would make everything so much less complicated.

They were going to work well together as a team in raising the boys. He was incredibly lucky that a woman like Melissa was the mother of his children.

He returned to the desk and tried to call her once again. When there was still no answer, the anxiety that had whispered through him screamed with alarm. Racing out of the study, he headed for the coat closet in the foyer and yanked out his coat. He grabbed his gun from the drawer and stuck it in his pocket.

"Henry? Where are you going?" Mary appeared in the foyer.

"I can't get hold of Melissa on the phone. Nobody answers and I've got a bad feeling."

Mary's hand flew up to her heart. "Maybe she was

in the bathroom, or stepped outside for a moment. Maybe she went to the office for something?"

"Maybe," he replied grimly. "But I won't be satisfied until I go there and check it out."

"Should I call Jimmy?" she asked worriedly.

"No, I'll call him if I need him. It's possible there's a perfectly logical explanation for her not answering the phone." He leaned over and kissed his mother on the cheek. "Don't worry."

"You'll call me?"

"The minute I get there and know that everything is all right." He didn't wait for her reply, but instead braced himself and hurried out into the cold evening air.

Minutes later as he pointed his truck toward town, he thought of all the logical explanations for the unanswered calls. Maybe she'd gone to get ice. Maybe one of the boys had been crying and she hadn't heard the ring of the phone.

There could be a dozen innocent reasons, but the possibility of those wasn't what made his heart bang in his chest. And his heart was banging fast and furious. He felt as if a wild beast had been let loose in his chest.

Fear. Rich and raw, it clawed at his guts, made him sick with worry. He'd never felt like this before. He'd never known this kind of fear.

The going was slow as the roads were slick and nasty. His hands clenched the steering wheel tightly as he prayed that nothing was wrong, that nothing bad had happened.

A lump lodged in the back of his throat. Had one of

the boys gotten ill and Melissa had somehow taken them to a doctor? Surely if that had happened, she would have called him.

By the time he reached the city limits he was almost nauseous with worry. Ed's Motel was on the south side of town along the main highway. It was a typical one-story building with connecting rooms that faced the parking lot. The office was in the center, but Henry went past it. He knew Melissa was in Room 112 and it was in front of that unit that he pulled up and parked.

He cut the engine and jumped out, his heart banging faster than he could ever remember it beating before. "Melissa?" He banged on the door. "Melissa, it's Henry. Open the door."

Nothing. No answer, no door opening. Absolutely nothing. He hammered on the door with his fist, then tried the door. It opened into a dark room.

He flipped on the light. The bedspread was wrinkled with pillows lined up against one side, but there was no suitcase, no babies and no Melissa anywhere in the room.

Maybe he got the room number wrong, he thought, but even as he grabbed onto that idea, he smelled the faint familiar scent of Melissa lingering in the air. She'd been here. Oh, God, so, where was she now?

He wouldn't have thought his heart could beat any faster, but it did, thundering in his chest with painful intensity.

He left the room and ran across the parking lot to the diner. Maybe she'd decided to take the boys there for dinner. Although he couldn't imagine her packing them up and carrying them across the way when the diner would deliver whatever she needed, he clung to the hope that this was the explanation for her absence.

Although on a normal evening at this time the diner would be packed, the weather conditions had the place nearly deserted. Henry took two steps inside the door and instantly knew she wasn't there.

His heart crashed to the floor. He stepped back outside and pulled his cell phone from his pocket. His fingers trembled as he punched in Jimmy's phone number.

"Jimmy, it's me," he said when the sheriff answered. "I need you to meet me at Ed's Motel. Something has happened to Melissa and the boys."

With Jimmy's assurance that he'd be right over, Henry walked back to the motel and into the office. Maybe he'd gotten the room number wrong. Maybe he'd only imagined the scent of Melissa in the room.

The owner, Ed Warren, was at the front desk and greeted Henry with a friendly smile.

"Henry, didn't expect to see you tonight," he said.

"Ed, that room I rented from you by phone. What room number was it?"

"112," Ed replied without hesitation. "I know because it's the only room I've rented in the past couple of days. This damned weather has practically closed me down. Why? Is there a problem?"

"Have you noticed anybody around the room? Have you seen a car or anything parked in front of it?"

"No, to be honest I haven't moved from behind this desk all day. I know a pretty lady came in for the key last night and that's all."

"The pretty lady isn't there now and she had a couple of babies with her. You haven't seen them this evening?"

Ed shook his head. "Sorry, Henry. I can't help you."

Henry reeled back out the door, almost blinded by the sickness that welled up inside him. Where were his babies? And where was Melissa?

Chapter 12

Melissa had never known such terror. There was no escape. She couldn't open the car door and jump out, not leaving Joey and James still in the car with Charlie. She was trapped and she had no idea why this was happening, what Charlie had planned for them.

As they left the city limits and began to travel on dark, lonely country roads, the terror clawed up the back of her throat and twisted her insides.

Joey and James had fallen asleep, unaware of the drama taking place. "Where are you taking us?" she finally asked, her voice reed thin.

"Don't you worry about it," Charlie replied. "If you

do what I tell you to do then there's no reason anybody has to get hurt and you and your kids will be fine."

"What do you want, Charlie? Why are you doing this?" She needed to make sense of it. "Is this because of your sister? Because Henry didn't want to marry her?"

Charlie laughed, the sound not pleasant. "I don't give a damn about Hilary. That stupid bitch dated Henry for over a year and couldn't close the deal. If she'd gotten Henry to marry her then I would have been on easy street. As Henry's brother-in-law I wouldn't have been shoveling horse crap anymore. I could have worked a respectable job with all the perks. Now I have to take matters into my own hands."

Henry had believed that somebody on the town council was responsible for the attacks on him. But he'd been wrong. "You were trying to kill Henry?" she asked.

Charlie glanced at her and laughed once again. "Trust me, if I'd wanted Henry dead, he'd be dead. I just wanted to disrupt his perfect little life, make him go to bed at night a little nervous."

"But why? What's he ever done to you?"

"I hate him!" Charlie exclaimed with vehemence. "I should be living his life. I should have his money. All he did to earn it was be born. I've been working my ass off for all my life. I came from nothing, but those babies in the backseat are my ticket to something."

It all crystallized in Melissa's mind. Kidnapped. Charlie was kidnapping her and the boys and was going to demand a ransom.

Henry had spent his entire life worrying that some woman might try to take his money from him and now because of her and the boys his fear was coming true, except it wasn't a woman about to take him, but a madman.

What if he didn't pay? Even as the possibility entered her mind she dismissed it. She'd only spent a couple of days with Henry, but she knew the man he was, she knew what was in his heart. He'd turn his bank account inside out to assure the safety of his children.

But what if something went terribly wrong? What if Charlie snapped or things didn't go as he planned? There was no question that to Charlie she and the boys were expendable. Nobody knew where they were, nobody would suspect Charlie of wanting to hurt Henry or having anything to do with her disappearance.

They were in mortal danger and at the moment she saw no way out of it. Maybe when they arrived to wherever he was taking them she'd be able to do something—anything—to get away. She grabbed on to that hope, that somehow, someway, she'd be able to figure out a plan.

She glanced at her wristwatch. It was just after six. Henry had said he'd call her sometime this evening. Had he tried to call? Did he even know they were missing yet?

It seemed like they drove forever before Charlie finally pulled to a stop. In the glare of the headlights stood a small shanty. It was dark and isolated, surrounded by trees laden with snow. There wasn't a light from a neighbor or a sign of civilization anywhere.

A shudder worked through Melissa, a shiver that had nothing to do with the cold as Charlie opened his car door. "Get the kids and don't try anything stupid. You're worth nothing to him or to me and I won't hesitate to kill you if you give me any trouble."

She believed him. The coldness in his eyes, the hardness in his voice let her know he meant what he said. Charlie knew Henry would pay whatever the demand to get his children back, but she was definitely expendable. Henry didn't love her.

She was grateful that the boys didn't awaken as she unfastened them and pulled them from the car seats. She held them tight as Charlie motioned her into the shanty with the barrel of his gun. Once inside he turned on a light that illuminated the dismal interior.

There was a sink, a small refrigerator, a two-burner hot plate, a microwave and a small table along one wall. On the other side of the small room was a single-size cot and a door she assumed led to a bathroom. A small electric heater blew warm air, but not enough to heat the entire room.

"Put the kids on the bed," he commanded.

On trembling legs she moved to the cot and gently placed the sleeping twins in the center of the small area. Tears blurred her vision as she straightened up and turned to face her captor.

"Unfortunately this is going to be your home away

from home for the next day or two," he said. "Sit down." He pointed to one of the chairs at the table.

With one backward glance at the sleeping twins Melissa did as he asked. "You threw that bomb through the window, didn't you?" she asked and was appalled by the quiver in her voice.

Charlie opened the cabinet beneath the sink and pulled out a heavy chain. The sight of it shot a new wave of fear through her. "Yeah, it's amazing how easy it is to build a little pipe bomb. I shot out the tire on Henry's car, too. My original plan was to waylay you as you left town, but Henry's decision to move you into the motel made it all so easy."

He straightened and locked one end of the chain on a metal hook that had been driven into the wall and then approached her with the other end.

"Please, you don't have to do this," she said, the tears not only blurring her vision but running hot down her cheeks. "I can talk to Henry. I'm sure he'll give you whatever you want. Just please, let me and my babies go."

"Shut up," he said. He bent down and grabbed her ankle. She instinctively kicked at him, the survival instinct roaring to life.

He stepped back from her, the gun pointed at her head. "Don't make this difficult. I told you that if you cooperate, you won't get hurt. But I won't hesitate to put a bullet through your head if you give me any trouble. You understand?"

She drew a deep breath, gulped back a sob and

nodded. She didn't want to give him a reason to kill her. She had to stay alive. She had to figure out a way out of this and save her boys.

"Now, I'm going to put this chain on your ankle. There's enough length for you to move around the room, take care of the kids and use the bathroom. There's some grub in the refrigerator and you should be fine until I get back here."

He fastened the chain around her ankle and she shuddered at the cold bite of steel against her skin. "I'll bring in your things so you should have everything you need."

With that he disappeared out the door. Instantly Melissa grabbed the chain in her hands and began to attempt to pull it out of the wall. She yanked and pulled, but there was no give at all.

She quickly dropped the chain as Charlie came back in carrying her suitcase and the diaper bag. The one thing he didn't have was her purse with her cell phone inside.

"Don't look so worried. You should only be here a couple of days, however long it takes him to get the cash for me. I'm not even going to make a ransom demand until tomorrow. I'll give him a night to worry. It will put him in a better mood to deal with me and my demands."

"Please, Charlie," she said one last time. "If you let us go now I won't tell anyone what you did."

"If and when you get a chance to tell anyone I'll be

long gone. I'll be a rich man on some tropical beach living under a new name."

"Henry will never stop looking for you," she insisted. "He'll hunt you down wherever you go. You'll live your life looking over your shoulder."

He smiled, obviously not concerned by her words. "But what a great life it's going to be. I'll be back later." He dropped the suitcase and diaper bag to the floor, then left the shanty. She heard him lock the door from the outside and then she was alone with just her sleeping babies to keep her company.

"Henry, there's no sign of a struggle or forced entry," Jimmy said. He'd arrived at the motel room with two of his deputies. "There's nothing to indicate that anything bad happened her. Maybe she just went home."

"Without her car?" The urgent burn in Henry's gut had only intensified over the past half an hour.

"Maybe she had somebody pick her up," Ben Whitfield, one of the deputies, said.

Henry shook his head. "She wouldn't have done that. She wouldn't have left without telling me goodbye."

"Maybe the scene at your house last night scared her more than she let on. Maybe she was afraid to tell you she was going home because she was afraid you'd try to change her mind," Jimmy said.

A new sick feeling swept through Henry. Had he been pushing her so hard the past couple of days that she might have taken off without telling him? Afraid that he'd push her to do something she didn't want to do? Even though their time together had been relatively brief, he believed he knew the kind of woman Melissa was and he was convinced that wasn't the case.

"I'm telling you, Jimmy, something's happened. We've got to find her." He looked at the sheriff. "She's in trouble. I know it. I feel it."

"Ben, you and Jake hit the streets, see if you can find anyone who might have seen something," Jimmy said.

"What about Tom Burke?" Henry asked.

"I already checked with Gordon. Tom is home with his family and can't have had anything to do with Melissa or your boys."

Henry grabbed Jimmy by the shoulder. "We have to do something, man. We have to find them." The emotions that filled Henry left him weak, a combination of the worst fear he'd ever known in his life.

"We'll find them, Henry. Why don't you go home and wait. Maybe she'll call."

"I can't go home. I need to do something," he said in frustration.

"Henry, take a deep breath. We don't even know that something bad has happened," Jimmy repeated.

But Henry knew. He felt it in his gut. There was no way that Melissa would have left town without speaking to him, no way she would have left her car at his house and taken off with somebody.

Something was wrong.

Something was horribly wrong.

"I'm going to drive around and see if anyone has seen her," Henry said. He couldn't go home and tell his mother that Melissa and the boys were missing.

Telling Jimmy he'd be in touch, Henry got into his truck and started to drive down the street, looking for anyone who might have seen Melissa and the boys. For the next hour he stopped at each and every business that was open and questioned anyone he found in the place.

Where could they be? What had happened in that motel room? Jimmy was right, there had been no sign of a struggle. Whoever she left with, she'd apparently gone willingly.

Surely if she'd planned on having somebody pick her up and take her back to Amarillo she would have said something to him when they'd spoken earlier on the phone. She would have made arrangements to get her car.

It was almost nine when he finally headed back to the ranch. He didn't know what else to do, where else to look. He only knew the terror that filled his heart.

The drive back to his place was the longest he'd ever made. Tears burned behind his eyes but he refused to let them fall. Tears implied sadness, grief and he absolutely refused to grieve for Melissa and the boys. He needed to stay strong.

His mother met him at the door. "What's going on?"

"They're gone." The words fell from his lips and suddenly the tears that he'd fought so hard to control spilled from him.

"Melissa and the boys aren't at the motel. We can't find them, Mom. We don't know where they are."

Mary reached for him and wrapped her arms around him, attempting to comfort him like she had when he'd been a little boy and had skinned his knee. But he wasn't a little boy and this was far worse than a bruised knee.

He stuffed back his tears and straightened. "I don't know what to do. I don't know what's happened. I've never felt so helpless in my life."

He allowed his mother to lead him into the living room, where they both sagged down to the sofa. "Jimmy and a couple of his men are out looking. I drove up and down the streets and asked everyone I saw, but nobody had seen them."

"Maybe she called a friend," Mary said, but Henry could tell by her tone that she didn't believe her own words.

"You and I both know she wouldn't have left town without telling us goodbye. That's not who Melissa is." He leaned his head back and closed his eyes and prayed that somehow this nightmare would end.

Both he and Mary jumped as the doorbell rang. Henry shot up off the sofa and raced to the door. He opened it to see Charlie.

"I just heard," Charlie said. "Is there anything I can do to help?"

Henry motioned him inside the foyer. "Last night when you dropped Melissa off at the motel did you see anybody around?"

Charlie frowned. "Not that I noticed. I made sure we weren't followed when we left here. I can't be a hundred percent certain that nobody saw her when I let her and the boys out of the car. God, man. What can I do?"

Henry raked a hand through his hair. "I don't think there's anything anyone can do at the moment. Jimmy and his men are out searching in town and I don't know what else to do."

"I'm heading home. You'll call me if I can do anything?"

"Thanks, Charlie. I will." Henry watched as the man left the house and walked to his vehicle in the driveway.

The night was dark and cold and Melissa was out there with his babies. "Maybe we scared her away," his mother spoke from behind him.

He turned to look at her.

"Maybe we came on too strong. We bought so many things, made it look as if we were making a home here for the twins." Mary wrung her hands together. "Maybe she's afraid you'll take those babies from her and so she ran away."

"No, she wouldn't do that." He knew in his heart, in the depths of his very soul, that she wouldn't just disappear. He turned back to the door and stared outside. "I think somebody has them. I think somebody took them from the motel room."

"But why?" Mary cried.

Once again he turned to face her. "Maybe as a final attempt to make me pull out of the election. I don't know. We won't know for sure until whoever has them contacts us."

"Surely whoever has them wouldn't hurt them." Mary's voice trembled with her fear.

He didn't attempt to give her false pacification. "I don't know, Mom."

"So, what do we do now?" she asked.

Henry's stomach clenched. "We wait."

Melissa wasted no time the minute Charlie left the shanty. First she worked to try to get the chain off her ankle. He'd secured it with a padlock and she was hoping maybe she could use something to pick it open. But a search of the two drawers in the kitchen area yielded nothing more than two spoons. Even the handle of the spoon was no good in trying to pick the lock.

The boys remained sleeping soundly. She was grateful for their silence. She needed to think. Even if she did manage to get herself free from the chain, then what? She had no idea where they were, no idea how far she'd have to walk with the twins in her arms to get help.

But she figured her odds were better braving the elements than staying here until Charlie returned. Henry had said that his breakup with Hilary hadn't seemed to matter to Charlie. Apparently, it had.

Charlie had seen Hilary and Henry's marriage as a ticket for him off the ranch. When that had fallen apart, she'd made the mistake of coming here and giving

Charlie a new bargaining chip. She glanced at the twins. No, two bargaining chips, she thought.

What scared her more than anything was that she didn't think Charlie intended to let her live. The twins couldn't identify their kidnappers, but she could. If she died then Charlie would be safe. He'd never have to look over his shoulder to see if somebody was after him.

For the next hour she pulled on the place where the chain was connected to the wall, hoping to break it loose. She finally sat on the floor, exhausted by her efforts and overwhelmed with defeat.

Silently she began to weep. She would never see her babies grow up. She'd never see their first step or hear them say Mommy. She wouldn't be there to put them on the bus for their first day of school, to straighten a tie when they went to their first school dance.

Pain flooded her as she stuffed a hand against her mouth to keep the sobs from ripping out of her. She wept until there were no more tears to weep and then she prayed. She prayed that no matter what happened to her, the boys would be safe. She prayed that they would live a long and happy life with Henry and Mary.

Thoughts of Henry brought more tears. She'd never see him again. She'd never see that slow slide of a sexy grin across his lips, the simmering sparkle of pleasure in his eyes.

Surely by now he knew they were missing. She looked at her watch. Almost ten. He would have called the room and gotten worried when she hadn't answered.

He was probably looking for her now. Unfortunately there was no way he'd ever suspect his right-hand man on the ranch, the worker he depended on. The last person he'd suspect would be Charlie.

She pulled herself up and looked in the cabinets, seeking something that could be used as a weapon. He might intend to kill her, but she'd like to be able to hurt him before he did. She'd like to be able to mark him in a way that might bring up some questions.

Her fingernails were kept too short to do damage to his face. But surely she could use something in the cabinets.

She searched every nook and cranny on the room and found nothing. The cabinets held only a handful of canned goods, some soup and pork and beans and corn. The refrigerator had a gallon of milk, a loaf of bread, a package of bologna and a small jar of mayo. The freezer contained five frozen dinners.

She had a feeling the food had been brought in specifically for her and there was just enough for a couple of days. This hadn't been a spur-of-the-moment decision on Charlie's part. He'd planned this and that depressed her even more.

Finally, she sat next to the bed where the twins slept and laid her head back. She could smell her babies, the sweet scent of innocence and love.

She closed her eyes with the weary knowledge that at least she knew they'd be loved by Henry for the rest of their lives, even if she wasn't around to share it.

Chapter 13

"Henry, Hilary is on the phone," Mary said.

Henry frowned. "I don't have time to talk to her now. Tell her I'll call her back later." He returned his attention to Jimmy, who sat on the chair opposite the sofa where Henry was seated.

"We're treating the motel room as a crime scene," Jimmy said. "Even though we don't know if a crime has occurred. I've got a couple of my boys lifting prints to see what we find."

"It's a motel room. You're probably going to find the prints of people who stayed there ten years ago," Henry said with a weary sigh.

"Ed's place is pretty clean. It's possible we'll lift fresh prints."

"And then what? Unless you have a matching set on file the prints won't tell us anything."

"Henry, we're doing the best we can," Jimmy replied patiently.

"I know, I know. You tell Tom Burke that if he had anything to do with this, then he wins. If he'll let them go unharmed, I'll leave him alone. I'll pull out of the race for mayor and he can continue his business practices as he sees fit."

"Henry, I don't think it's Tom," Jimmy said. "Or anyone he's hired. I've known Tom for most of my life. Sure, he's a scoundrel, he's a white-color criminal but this isn't something he's capable of."

"Would you stake Melissa's life on that? Stake the lives of my boys on it?" Henry replied.

"Of course not. I'm just telling you what my gut is telling me and that's that Tom isn't responsible."

"Then who is?" Henry asked as a hollowness threatened to swallow him whole. "Jesus, Jimmy, who is responsible? Who could hate me this much?"

Jimmy swiped his broad hand down the length of his face. "I don't know. It might not be about hate. It might be about greed. If this is some kind of kidnapping then I'm guessing that you'll hear from the kidnapper."

Henry looked at his watch. It was after ten. "We don't even know how long they've been missing. I spoke to her this morning but didn't speak to her after that."

"I checked with the diner. Dinner was delivered to the room at around four-thirty so we know she and the boys were there then," Jimmy said.

"I've made coffee," Mary said as she stepped into the living room.

Jimmy stood. "Come on, Henry, let's go have some coffee. It looks like it's going to be a long night."

The last thing Henry wanted was to sit around and drink coffee while Melissa and his boys were out there somewhere. He wanted to beat on every door in the town of Dalhart until he found the place where Melissa and the twins were being held.

But he followed Jimmy into the kitchen, where the two men sat at the table while his mother poured them each a cup of the fresh brew.

"Shouldn't we call the FBI or something?" Mary asked. She looked as if she'd aged ten years in the past couple of hours.

Jimmy shook his head. "They won't be interested until I have evidence that a crime has occurred. She's only been missing for five or six hours and we don't know if she made the decision to go missing of her own free will."

Henry frowned and wrapped his hands around his coffee cup, seeking the warmth to banish the icy chill that had taken possession of his body the moment he'd entered the empty motel room.

"If this is a kidnapping for ransom I wish to hell somebody would call me," Henry said.

They all froze as Jimmy's cell phone rang. Henry's stomach clenched as Jimmy answered. He listened for a moment. "Just keep me posted," he finally said then hung up. "That was Jake. He and Ben have questioned everyone in the block surrounding the motel and nobody has seen Melissa."

"Why doesn't he call?" Henry cried. "If somebody has them why in the hell haven't they called to tell me what he wants?"

The frustration, the fear and the rage that had been building throughout the night exploded and Henry slammed his hands down on the table. "If anybody hurts them I'll kill them. I swear, Jimmy. I'll kill the bastard responsible for this."

At that moment the doorbell rang. Henry leaped up from the table and hurried to the door, his heart thundering in the hope that it would be Melissa.

It wasn't. It was Hilary.

"Henry, I heard about Melissa and the babies missing. I need to talk to you." There was a trembling urgency in her voice.

"Hilary, this really isn't a good time," he said, unable to stop the crashing waves of pain that coursed through him.

She reached out and placed her hand on his shoulder. "Please, Henry, I think maybe I know who is responsible."

He stared at her, wondering if this was some crazy ploy to get close to him. "What are you talking about?"

He was aware of Jimmy and his mother stepping into the foyer.

"Charlie was real upset when we broke up. He thought if you and I got married then you'd get him a job that paid well, a job in a fancy office somewhere. A couple of days ago he told me he had plans to get enough money to blow this town and live the easy life. When I pressed him for details he refused to say anything more."

The words exploded out of her in a rush, along with a torrent of tears. "I might be a lot of things, Henry, but I saw the way you looked at Melissa, I saw the look in your eyes when you saw those babies and I can't condone this. I think Charlie has done something terrible and I just had to tell you."

Henry stared at her in confusion. Charlie? Henry's mind buzzed. Charlie knew where she was staying. Melissa would have trusted Charlie. She would have gone with him without questions. Still, he was reluctant to believe it. "But he was here just a little while ago. He offered his help."

"I'm just telling you what I think, Henry, and I think he has Melissa and the boys," Hilary said.

Henry pulled his cell phone from his pocket and punched in Charlie's phone number. His heart crawled into his throat as he heard it ring and ring. "There's no answer," he said as he clicked off.

"I know where Charlie lives," Jimmy said with a frown. "There's no way he could have Melissa and the twins stashed in that tiny little apartment of his. Somebody would hear the boys crying or would have seen him bring them all inside."

Henry was processing everything in the span of seconds. Charlie could have easily taken the shot at him when he'd been out riding in the pasture. Charlie would have known that Henry and Melissa had gone to town and would have known about when they would be returning home. Charlie, who then tramped through the snow to obscure his own footprints, could have easily tossed the pipe bomb through the window.

Charlie. He still had trouble wrapping his mind around it. Charlie had been his right-hand man, his go-to guy for everything around the ranch.

"Charlie has a little shack, a place he goes hunting. Maybe he has them there," Hilary said.

"Why? I trusted him. I've always treated him fairly," Henry said.

"I think he hates you, Henry. He envies you your money, your life and I think he knew how much you cared about Melissa and the boys, cared enough to pay whatever ransom he might come up with."

The slow simmering rage that had been building in Henry throughout the night once again rose to the surface. "Where's the shack?" he asked.

Hilary wiped her tears with the back of her hand. "I hope I'm not sending you on a wild-goose chase. I don't want anything to happen to Melissa or those precious babies."

"Where's the shack, Hilary?" he demanded. He suddenly felt like too much time had been wasted.

As Hilary gave them directions to the shack, Henry was already pulling on his coat. He grabbed his gun and looked at Jimmy expectantly.

"Let's go," Jimmy said with a nod. He looked at Hilary. "If Charlie contacts you, don't tell him you spoke to us. Don't say anything to warn him or I'll see you behind bars for obstruction of justice."

"Please be careful. I honestly don't know what he's capable of," she said.

As Henry stepped out into the cold dark night he had a last glance of Hilary reaching for his mother's hand. He hoped to hell she was telling the truth and he prayed that they wouldn't be too late.

Melissa was cold. She didn't know if it was because the little heater simply couldn't warm the interior of the cabin or if it was fear that had her freezing.

Waiting. Wondering what happened next, that was what had her blood icy in her veins.

She certainly couldn't sleep, although she was grateful that the boys slumbered soundly. Seeking internal warmth, she finally opened a can of tomato soup and emptied it into a pan, then set it on the hot plate to warm.

As she waited for it to heat she wondered if Charlie had contacted Henry, if he'd already demanded a king's ransom for the return of the boys. He'd said he'd wait until morning, but maybe he'd gotten impatient. She just wanted this over.

She winced as she stood to stir the soup. She'd worked so long at trying to get the chain off her ankle she'd made it bleed.

Maybe she should be sleeping. Maybe Charlie didn't intend to return tonight and she should be getting what little rest she could. But even as she thought that, she knew there was no way she could sleep. She wanted to hold her boys. She wanted to squeeze them to her heart. She wanted to hear James's belly laugh one last time, see Joey's sweet smile. She stirred the soup as tears began to course down her cheeks once again.

Henry, her heart cried. She would never see him again. The only thing she could hope was that he would tell the boys about her, about how much she'd loved them, about what a good mom she'd wanted to be.

She froze as she heard the sound of a vehicle approach. Headlight beams flashed into the window. Sheer terror leaped into her throat. Had the deal gone down? Had Charlie come back to kill her?

The footsteps on the porch sounded loud, like gunshots, and when the door opened Charlie came inside. "Hi, honey, I'm home." He snickered, as if finding the joke amusing.

Melissa turned away from the hot plate. "Have you contacted Henry?"

"Not yet. I told you I was going to give him a little time to worry. I just figured I needed to stop back here and check on my investment." He leaned against the door and looked down at her ankle. "Looks like you worked hard to get out of that. Short of chewing off your foot, you aren't going anywhere."

Melissa had never hated anyone as much as she hated him. She'd never believed herself capable of killing anyone, but she'd kill for her children and if she got the chance, she'd kill Charlie without a blink of her eyes.

He kicked out a chair and sat at the small table and she backed up against the cabinet. "You're going to kill me, aren't you?" She didn't wait for him to answer. "I won't tell that it was you. I'll say that I don't know who took us, that he wore a mask and I didn't recognize him."

She hated that she was begging for her life, but she wanted to live. She had all the reasons in the world to want to stay alive.

"Lady, I wouldn't trust you as far as I could throw you," he replied.

With those words Melissa knew that he had no intention of letting her live and a new wave of grief crashed through her.

She turned back to the soup at the same time the front door crashed in. She whirled back around and everything seemed to go in slow motion.

Henry stood at the door, bigger than life, his eyes wild and dangerous. At the same time Charlie jumped up and drew his gun and lifted it to point at him.

In an instant Melissa knew Henry was about to die. Without thinking, she picked up the pan of hot soup and threw it at Charlie. As it splashed across the back of his head, he yelled and his gun dropped to the floor. The twins began to cry as Henry let loose a thunderous roar and tackled Charlie to the floor.

Melissa kicked Charlie's gun under the bed, then ran to the twins as Henry and Charlie wrestled with each other. Her heart pounded as she pulled the screaming boys into her arms and watched the life-and-death battle between the man she loved and the man who would kill her.

A sob escaped her when Henry pressed his gun barrel into Charlie's temple, halting the fight. At that moment Jimmy burst into the room.

"I got it, Henry. Drop your gun," he said.

Henry didn't move. His handsome features were twisted into a mask of rage. His entire body trembled and it was obvious how badly he wanted to put a bullet through Charlie's head.

"Henry, don't do it," Jimmy said and touched Henry's shoulder. "Come on, man. Let him go. I'll take it from here."

Henry squeezed his eyes closed, the internal battle he was waging bringing a new fear to Melissa. She knew if he shot Charlie his life would never be the same. It might feel good at the moment but eventually it would destroy him.

"Henry." She spoke his name softly. He opened his eyes and met her gaze. In the depths of his eyes she saw the torture he'd suffered over the past couple of hours.

"Let Jimmy take him away. Please, I need your help with the boys."

With a strangled sob, he lowered his gun and rolled off Charlie. Jimmy immediately handcuffed Charlie and hauled him to his feet.

Henry rushed over to her and knelt in front of her. He cupped her face between his palms, his gaze intense. "Did he hurt you? Oh, God, did he hurt you or the boys?"

"No, I'm okay. We're all okay." The boys had begun to calm.

He glanced down at the chain around her ankle and as he tensed as if to spring up again, she grabbed his arm. "It's okay."

Henry turned to look at Charlie and Jimmy. "Search him, Jimmy. I need a key to get this chain off her."

A moment later he unlocked the chain and removed it from her ankle. As he gently rubbed her skin, she remembered how he'd rubbed her cold feet on the night that they had been snowbound together.

Then she was in his arms, weeping in the aftermath, and he held her tight, as if afraid to ever let her go again. Eventually he did let her go. Gordon arrived along with several other deputies who would process what was now part of a crime scene.

Jimmy left to take Charlie to jail and Melissa and Henry and the boys got into Gordon's patrol car so he could take them home.

The car seats were shifted from Charlie's vehicle to the back of Gordon's car and once the boys were settled in they immediately fell back asleep. Melissa sat between them, happy yet exhausted by the turmoil and the lateness of the hour.

As they drove home Henry told Melissa about Hilary telling them that she thought Charlie might be involved. When they got back to the house Mary and Hilary stepped out on the porch to greet them.

Henry carried the twins and when Melissa reached the porch Mary pulled her into a bone-crunching hug. "Thank God," she said. "Thank God you're all okay."

As Mary released her, Melissa grabbed Hilary's hands. "Thank you," she said to the beautiful woman. "You saved my life."

Tears shone in Hilary's eyes. "I'm so sorry. I can't believe he did this. I always knew Charlie had a mean streak, but I never knew he was capable of something like this." She pulled her hands from Melissa's. "I'm going home now. I'm sure you all need some time alone."

An hour later the twins were asleep in their beds upstairs and Jimmy arrived to take a statement from Melissa.

It was near dawn when Jimmy left and Mary led Melissa to one of the spare bedrooms. As they passed the boys' room she saw Henry sitting in a chair just inside the door, as if guarding the king's treasure. Daddy on duty, she thought, and knew he'd probably be in that chair until dawn.

Minutes later as she lay in bed, even though she was exhausted she couldn't shut off her mind. Not only did her brain whirl with all the events and emotions of the night, but thoughts of Henry also filled her head and her heart.

She needed to get home. She couldn't stay here any longer. She'd allowed him into her heart in a way no other man had ever been. Each and every moment she spent with him only deepened her love for him.

It was time to go.

Chapter 14

Henry felt sick.

She was leaving. They were leaving. Even though he'd known this time would come, he wasn't ready to tell them goodbye, even if it was just a temporary goodbye.

It was midafternoon and the sun shone through the window as she finished the last of her packing. "I hate to see you go," he said.

"I know, but it's not like this is a final goodbye." She shut her suitcase and smiled at him, but her smile looked forced. The sunshine found her hair and sparkled in it and a press of emotion rose up in Henry's chest. He swallowed against it, unsure why this was so difficult.

She pulled her suitcase off the bed and set it on the

floor. "I need some time at home, Henry." Her eyes weren't as bright as they usually were. "I need some time to process everything that's happened."

He nodded. "I know. At least we know now that there's no more danger here. The next time you come back things will be completely different. You'll have no reason to be afraid."

She gazed at him with an enigmatic expression on her face. "I'm just glad it's all over for you...for us."

"I'm sorry, Melissa. I'm so sorry that you and the boys were put in any danger."

She held up a hand to stop him. "Don't apologize. It wasn't your fault. You couldn't have known about Charlie. You have nothing to be sorry for." She glanced at her watch. "And now, I really need to get on the road."

He nodded and reluctantly picked up her suitcase. Together they went down the stairs, where Mary and the twins were in the living room.

"You'll come back, won't you?" Mary asked worriedly.

"Of course," Melissa replied. "And anytime you want you're welcome to come to Amarillo for a visit."

Mary smiled. "I might just surprise you."

"I'd love a visit from you," Melissa replied. She leaned down and picked up James from the blanket on the floor where they had been lying.

"I'll get Joey," Mary said. As she picked up the smiling little boy tears filled her eyes. She looked at Melissa and gave her a teary smile. "I don't know what's worse, saying goodbye to these precious boys or saying goodbye to you."

"I packed up some of the Christmas presents in the trunk," Henry said as they all left the house and walked to Melissa's car, and Mary put Joey in his car seat. "If you need or want anything else, just give me a call."

"We'll be fine," Melissa said, then leaned into the backseat to buckle James into his seat. When she straightened, her gaze held Henry's for a long moment.

In the blue depths of her eyes Henry saw words unspoken and a shine of emotion that momentarily stole his breath away. It was there only a moment, then gone.

"Thank you. Thank you both for your generosity," she said. Once again her gaze met Henry's and he thought she was going to say something more, but instead she slid into the driver's seat and waved goodbye.

As he watched her car disappear down the driveway, he was struck with the fiercest wave of loneliness he'd ever felt.

"You're a fool, Henry James Randolf," his mother exclaimed and started back into the house.

"What are you talking about? I didn't do anything," he said.

"That's right. And that's why you're a fool." She went into the front door and slammed it behind her.

Henry swiped a hand through his hair and sighed. Women. He'd never understand them. His mother was probably upset with him because he hadn't managed to talk Melissa into moving into the carriage house. But after the trauma she'd suffered the night before, he hadn't wanted to pressure her anymore about it.

There might be a time in the future to bring up the subject again. In the meantime he had some things to take care of that would hopefully take his mind off the empty ache inside his chest.

For the next three days Henry stayed as busy as he could. Everyone in town was stunned to hear what Charlie had done and Henry was shocked and warmed by the amount of support he received from friends and neighbors.

He also made a difficult apology to Tom Burke, who surprised him by saying he was resigning his position as city manager and he and his wife were moving to Florida.

It was each evening after his mother had gone to bed and he sat in his chair with a glass of scotch when thoughts of Melissa and the boys filled his head.

It was amazing how much they had imbued the house with warmth, with joy. He missed seeing her smile and hearing that musical laugh of hers as she teased him. He missed talking to her, just sharing moments of time that could never be recaptured again.

She was a wonderful woman and someday she'd make some man a wonderful wife. He couldn't help it that he wasn't the man to fill that role in her life.

He would be the best father that he could be, but that's all he had to offer her. He hadn't pretended to be anything else but what he was—a confirmed bachelor.

* * *

The time with Henry at his house had taken on the quality of a wonderful dream as Melissa threw herself back into her real life. The boys settled back into their normal routine as if they'd never been away from home and Melissa tried to do the same.

It was Thursday morning when she sat at her computer in her living room working to build a brand-new slick Web page to advertise her business.

The twins were on the living-room floor, babbling happily to her and to each other. At least they didn't appear any worse for the drama that had taken place in that little shanty. Even Melissa was surprised by how easily she'd managed to put it all behind her. She had a life to build and couldn't dwell on that night with Charlie and how close she'd come to losing everything.

She tried not to think too much about Henry. She was in his life by accident and she couldn't forget that. It hurt to think of him, to love him and know that she would always be the mother of his children but never the woman of his heart.

For the past four nights she'd spent hours on the Internet trying to reconnect with MysteryMom but she hadn't been able to find the woman in any of the chat rooms she'd visited or anywhere else. It was as if she'd been a figment of Melissa's imagination.

Melissa would have liked to tell her that she'd successfully united Joey and James with their daddy and in that respect the story had a happy ending.

And someday maybe Melissa would find her happy ending with a man who would love her, a man who wouldn't be able to wait to marry her. At the moment the idea of romance with anyone left a bad taste in her mouth. It would take her a while to heal, to get over the heartbreak of loving Henry.

At least he hadn't spoken again about her moving into the carriage house. If he brought it up again she was afraid she would confess that the reason she didn't want to live there was because she was in love with him. She didn't want to burden him with her love. The last thing she wanted to do was complicate their relationship.

It was important for the boys' sake that Henry and Melissa's relationship remain calm and pleasant, not filled with stress or tension.

She stopped working on the Web page at six and fed the boys a bottle, then snuggled with them on the sofa. This was the time of the evening when loneliness struck her the hardest.

As the twins got sleepy and fell silent, the quiet of the apartment pressed in on her. She couldn't help but remember those nights with Henry when they'd sat and talked and just shared little pieces of each other.

She had to make sure in the future she maintained an emotional distance from him. She was going to have to see him on a regular basis but somehow, someway, she had to uninvolve her heart where he was concerned.

When the boys had fallen asleep she carried them one at a time to the cribs in their small bedroom then returned to the living room. She sat back down at the computer, but her thoughts were still consumed by Henry. He'd called every day since she'd been home, short chats about the twins that had only made it more difficult for her to gain the emotional distance she needed from him.

He'd wanted her to drive back to Dalhart this weekend, but she'd told him that she wasn't ready to make the drive again. He'd been disappointed but seemed to understand and they'd made plans for him to come to her apartment the following weekend.

There was a motel nearby and he could stay there and when she went back to Dalhart she would stay at a motel and he could visit the twins there. It was important that she set boundaries when it came to the visitation. He was her weakness and it would be far too easy for her to fall into his bed if he wanted her every time they were together for visitation.

Even now as she thought about being with him, kissing him and making love with him, she was filled with a longing that knew no bounds.

She was just about to stop working on the Web page and turn on the television when a knock fell on her door. She opened the door and her breath caught in her throat.

Henry. He stood before her as if conjured up by her thought, by her deep longing for him. "Surprise," he said with a smile that looked distinctly uncomfortable.

"Henry… What are you doing here?" She opened the door to allow him inside and as he swept by her she caught the sweet familiar scent that belonged to him alone. She closed the door and turned to face him.

He looked wonderful in a pair of worn jeans and a flannel plaid shirt and his winter coat. He looked just like the sexy, handsome cowboy who had rescued her on that snowy night over a year ago.

"I couldn't wait until next weekend or the weekend after that," he said.

She frowned. "But you've come so late. The boys are already asleep for the night. You should have called and let me know you were coming."

He shrugged out of his coat and laid it across the back of the sofa. "I would have called, but I didn't know I was coming until I was in the car and on my way." He stared at her for a long moment, his gaze inscrutable. "We need to talk."

He seemed nervous and ill at ease and suddenly she was afraid. Had he come to tell her that he'd changed his mind, that he'd decided he was going to fight her for custody of the twins? Had being away from them made him decide he'd do anything to keep them with him?

"Talk about what?" She sank down on the sofa, afraid that her trembling legs wouldn't hold her up any longer. She motioned him into the chair opposite the sofa but he remained standing with his back against the door, as if he might escape at any moment.

"I want to talk to you about the carriage house," he said.

"Henry, I…"

He held up a hand to stop her from saying anything

more. "Please, just listen to me for a minute. I've never offered something to somebody and then taken it back, but that's what I'm doing now. I don't want you to live in the carriage house."

Even though she hadn't intended to move in there, his words shot a sliver of pain through her. He didn't want her there. He didn't want her that close to him.

She nodded and told herself it was for the best. It hadn't been something she wanted to do anyway. "Okay," she replied.

"No, it's not okay. Nothing has been okay since you and the boys left." He shoved off from the door and walked the width of the room to stand in front of her. He stared at her, his expression impossible to read.

He finally drew a deep breath. "I thought I had my life all figured out, then you arrived with the boys and everything got all screwed up."

"I'm sorry. It was never my intention to mess up your life," she replied. Could this get more horrible? She fought back the sting of tears, refusing to allow him to see the depth of emotion inside her where he was concerned.

With one smooth movement he sat next to her. "My mother told me that my father might have done me a disservice in pounding into my head that all any woman would ever want from me was my money. Certainly my relationship with Hilary proved him right."

"But he was wrong, Henry," Melissa exclaimed fervently. "You're a wonderful man and you'd be a wonderful man with or without your money."

He smiled then, that slow sexy grin that would always have the capacity to warm her. "Last night I was sitting in the living room alone and thinking about the boys and what the future might hold. When I thought about them mounting a horse for the very first time, you were there in my vision. When I visualized putting them on the bus for their first day of school, in my vision you were standing beside me and holding my hand. Each and every fantasy of the future I imagined had you in it."

He frowned and his gaze never left hers. "And it wasn't just the boys' future that I fantasized about. I thought about your laughter and the way your eyes light up when you're happy. I thought about sleeping next to you, making love to you and I realized there was no way I wanted you living a separate life in the carriage house. I don't want you dating. I don't want you to be alone."

She didn't say a word. She was afraid she was misinterpreting what he was telling her. She remained frozen, her gaze locked with his.

"I realize now why it's been so easy for me to be a confirmed bachelor," he continued. "It's because I'd never met a woman I wanted to share my life with, a woman I loved mindlessly, desperately, until I met you."

Melissa's heart soared. "I wasn't going to move into the carriage house because I'm in love with you and I couldn't live there and see you every day and not be a real part of your life."

Her words seemed to break something loose in Henry. His eyes flared bright and he reached out and placed his palm against her cheek. "God, I was hoping you'd say something like that."

"I love you, Henry, but are you sure your feelings for me aren't because of the boys?"

"Melissa, I love you as the mother of my children, but my love doesn't begin and end there. I love you because you're strong and beautiful. I love you because you make me feel like I've never felt before in my life. I want to spend my life with you. Marry me, Melissa. Marry me and move into my house. Let us be a real family together."

His mouth took hers in a kiss that tasted of desire, but more it tasted of the future, of promises made and kept and the family she'd always wanted.

"You haven't answered me," he said when he finally pulled his mouth from hers. "Will you marry me? Will you share the rest of your life with me?"

"Yes," she replied breathlessly. "Yes! Yes!"

He pulled her into his arms and she leaned her head against his chest, listening to the strong beat of his heart.

"I wonder if MysteryMom has any idea what she's managed to accomplish?" she said.

"I have a feeling she knows," he replied. "I'll give you the world, Melissa. Whatever you want, whatever you need to be happy."

"I don't need or want anything but you and the boys," she replied.

"There is one thing you can eventually give me, if you're willing."

She rose up and looked at him. "What on earth could I possibly give you that you don't already have?"

He smiled, his eyes lit with love. "Twin daughters."

Melissa's heart swelled inside her. She was filled with such love, such joy, that she couldn't find her voice. She could only nod as he once again claimed her mouth with his.

She would forever be grateful for the blizzard that had brought them together on that night so long ago and to a woman named MysteryMom who had led her to happiness that she knew was going to last a lifetime.

Epilogue

She sat in front of her computer and stared at the e-mail she'd just written, but hesitated in hitting the button that would send the message on its way.

MysteryMom picked up the cup of coffee sitting next to her at the desk and took a sip, her mind whirling with the words she'd just typed.

It was amazing what kind of information could be gained when money was no object and you had contacts everywhere in the world. For the past year she'd used those contacts and her money for a mission—the mission of uniting people for the sake of their children.

It had begun when she'd started dropping in on various chat rooms and began to hear stories about women who didn't know where the father of their children were or how to get in touch with them to let them know they were fathers.

The stories had torn at her heart until finally she'd decided to try to do something—use her resources to bring some sort of reunion to the men and women who had parented children.

So far she'd been successful with several couples, but this one worried her. She reread the e-mail she'd composed and thought of the man and woman involved.

A terrible fate had pulled Emily Grainger and Jagger Holtz apart after a single night together. The result of that night had been a daughter named Michelle.

MysteryMom now had the pieces of the puzzle that could potentially bring together Emily and Jagger. She knew the information contained in the e-mail could save a man's life, but might also bring extreme danger to both him and Emily.

He's already in danger, she thought to herself. And if the e-mail wasn't sent then in all probability he would die.

She owed it to Jagger Holtz to send the e-mail and she prayed that when she did Emily Grainer would survive whatever consequences might come.

Drawing in a deep breath, the woman who called herself MysteryMom hit the send button.

* * * * *

Don't miss the next
TOP SECRET DELIVERIES *romance:*
THE SOLDIER'S SECRET DAUGHTER,
by Cindy Dees.
Available December 2009.

Celebrate 60 years of pure reading pleasure
with Harlequin®!
Just in time for the holidays,
Silhouette Special Edition® is proud to present
New York Times *bestselling author*
Kathleen Eagle's
ONE COWBOY, ONE CHRISTMAS

Rodeo rider Zach Beaudry was a travelin' man—
until he broke down in middle-of-nowhere South
Dakota during a deep freeze. That's when an
angel came to his rescue….

"Don't die on me. Come on, Zel. You know how much I love you, girl. You're all I've got. Don't do this to me here. Not *now.*"

But Zelda had quit on him, and Zach Beaudry had no one to blame but himself. He'd taken his sweet time hitting the road, and then miscalculated a shortcut. For all he knew he was a hundred miles from gas. But even if they were sitting next to a pump, the ten dollars he had in his pocket wouldn't get him out of South Dakota, which was not where he wanted to be right now. Not even his beloved pickup truck, Zelda, could get him much of anywhere on fumes. He was sitting out in the cold in the middle of nowhere. And getting colder.

He shifted the pickup into Neutral and pulled hard on the steering wheel, using the downhill slope to get her off the blacktop and into the roadside grass, where she shuddered to a standstill. He stroked the padded dash. "You'll be safe here."

But Zach would not. It was getting dark, and it was already too damn cold for his cowboy ass. Zach's battered body was a barometer, and he was feeling South Dakota, big-time. He'd have given his right arm to be climbing into a hotel hot tub instead of a brutal blast of north wind. The right was his free arm anyway. Damn thing had lost altitude, touched some part of the bull and caused him a scoreless ride last time out.

It wasn't scoring him a ride this night, either. A carload of teenagers whizzed by, topping off the insult by laying on the horn as they passed him. It was at least twenty minutes before another vehicle came along. He stepped out and waved both arms this time, damn near getting himself killed. Whatever happened to *do unto others?* In places like this, decent people didn't leave each other stranded in the cold.

His face was feeling stiff, and he figured he'd better start walking before his toes went numb. He struck out for a distant yard light, the only sign of human habitation in sight. He couldn't tell how distant, but he knew he'd be hurting by the time he got there, and he was counting on some kindly old man to be answering the door. No shame among the lame.

It wasn't like Zach was fresh off the operating table—

it had been a few months since his last round of repairs—but he hadn't given himself enough time. He'd lopped a couple of weeks off the near end of the doc's estimated recovery time, rigged up a brace, done some heavy-duty taping and climbed onto another bull. Hung in there for five seconds—four seconds past feeling the pop in his hip and three seconds short of the buzzer.

He could still feel the pain shooting down his leg with every step. Only this time he had to pick the damn thing up, swing it forward and drop it down again on his own.

Pride be damned, he just hoped *somebody* would be answering the door at the end of the road. The light in the front window was a good sign.

The four steps to the covered porch might as well have been four hundred, and he was looking to climb them with a lead weight chained to his left leg. His eyes were just as screwed up as his hip. Big black spots danced around with tiny red flashers, and he couldn't tell what was real and what wasn't. He stumbled over some shrubbery, steadied himself on the porch railing and peered between vertical slats.

There in the front window stood a spruce tree with a silver star affixed to the top. Zach was pretty sure the red sparks were all in his head, but the white lights twinkling by the hundreds throughout the huge tree, those were real. He wasn't too sure about the woman hanging the shiny balls. Most of her hair was caught up on her head and fastened in a curly clump, but the light captured by the escaped bits crowned her with a golden halo. Her face was a soft shadow, her body a willowy silhouette beneath a long white gown. If this was where the mind ran off to when cold started shutting down the rest of the body, then Zach's final worldly thought was, *This ain't such a bad way to go.*

If she would just turn to the window, he could die looking into the eyes of a Christmas angel.

* * * * *

*Could this woman from Zach's past get the lonesome
cowboy to come in from the cold…for good?
Look for
ONE COWBOY, ONE CHRISTMAS
by Kathleen Eagle
Available December 2009 from
Silhouette Special Edition®*

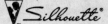

SPECIAL EDITION

**FROM *NEW YORK TIMES* AND *USA TODAY*
BESTSELLING AUTHOR**

KATHLEEN EAGLE

ONE COWBOY,
One Christmas

When bull rider Zach Beaudry appeared
out of thin air on Ann Drexler's ranch,
she thought she was seeing a ghost of
Christmas past. And though Zach had
no memory of their night of passion years
ago, they were about to share a future
he would never forget.

*Available December 2009
wherever books are sold.*

SSE65493

Visit Silhouette Books at www.eHarlequin.com

REQUEST YOUR FREE BOOKS!

2 FREE NOVELS PLUS 2 FREE GIFTS!

Silhouette® Romantic SUSPENSE

Sparked by Danger, Fueled by Passion!

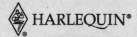

HARLEQUIN®

American ★ Romance®

A Cowboy Christmas
MARIN THOMAS

2 stories in 1!

The holidays are a rough time for widower
Logan Taylor and single dad Fletcher McFadden—
neither hunky cowboy has been lucky in love.
But Christmas is the season of miracles! Logan
meets his match in "A Christmas Baby," while
Fletcher gets a second chance at love in "Marry
Me, Cowboy." This year both cowboys are on
Santa's Nice list!

*Available December
wherever books are sold.*

"LOVE, HOME & HAPPINESS"

HARLEQUIN
Ambassadors

Want to share your passion for reading Harlequin® Books?

Become a Harlequin Ambassador!

Harlequin Ambassadors are a group of passionate and well-connected readers who are willing to share their joy of reading Harlequin® books with family and friends.

You'll be sent all the tools you need to spark great conversation, including free books!

All we ask is that you share the romance with your friends and family!

You'll also be invited to have a say in new book ideas and exchange opinions with women just like you!

To see if you qualify* to be a Harlequin Ambassador, please visit www.HarlequinAmbassadors.com.

*Please note that not everyone who applies to be a Harlequin Ambassador will qualify. For more information please visit www.HarlequinAmbassadors.com.

Thank you for your participation.

BAP09BPA

Silhouette Desire

New York Times Bestselling Author

SUSAN MALLERY

HIGH-POWERED, HOT-BLOODED

Innocently caught up in a corporate scandal, schoolteacher
Annie McCoy has no choice but to take the tempting deal offered
by ruthless CEO Duncan Patrick. Six passionate months later,
Annie realizes Duncan will move on, with or without her. Now
all she has to do is convince him she is the one he really wants!

Available December 2009 wherever you buy books.

ALWAYS POWERFUL, PASSIONATE AND PROVOCATIVE

Visit Silhouette Books at www.eHarlequin.com

SD76981

Silhouette®

Romantic

SUSPENSE

COMING NEXT MONTH

Available November 24, 2009

#1587 THE CAVANAUGH CODE—Marie Ferrarella
Cavanaugh Justice
When detective Taylor McIntyre discovers a suspicious man lurking around a crime scene, she never guesses he'll be her new partner on the case. But the moment J. C. Laredo sweeps into the squad room, Taylor can't deny the attraction she feels for the P.I. As they work the nights away, growing ever closer to catching the killer, will they finally give in to the love that's been building inside?

#1588 THE SOLDIER'S SECRET DAUGHTER—Cindy Dees
Top Secret Deliveries
Her mystery man disappeared after their one night of passion, but he left Emily Grainger with a constant reminder—their daughter. So when she receives a tip that leads her to a ship's container, she's shocked to discover her long-lost love held captive inside! Now on the run from his captors, Jagger Holtz will do anything to protect his newly discovered family.

#1589 SEDUCED BY THE OPERATIVE—Merline Lovelace
Code Name: Danger
The president's daughter is having strange dreams, and psychologist Claire Cantwell has been tasked with finding their cause. In a desperate race against time, she and Colonel Luis Esteban follow a mysterious trail halfway around the world. As they face a lethal killer, can they also learn to face their own demons and give in to the love they clearly feel for each other?

#1590 PROTECTING THEIR BABY—Sheri WhiteFeather
Warrior Society
After her first and only one-night stand, Lisa Gordon suddenly finds herself pregnant...and in danger. Rex Sixkiller enjoys his free-spirited life, but when Lisa and his unborn child are threatened, he takes action. As the threats escalate and Rex fights to keep them safe, he and Lisa also wage a losing battle to protect their hearts.

SRSCNMBPA1109